LITTLE BASTARD

SIMON CORBIN

Copyright © 2015 Simon Corbin

First Edition

ISBN-13: 978-1522771371

ISBN-10: 1522771379

All rights reserved under the International and Pan-American Copyright Conventions. No part of this book may be reproduced or transmitted in any form or by any means, electronic or mechanical, including photocopying, recording, or by any information storage and retrieval system, without permission in writing from the publisher.

This is a work of fiction. Names, places, businesses, characters, and incidents, are either the product of the author's imagination or are used fictitiously, and any resemblance to any actual persons, living or dead, organizations, events or locales, or any other entity, is entirely coincidental.

Warning: the unauthorized reproduction or distribution of this copyrighted work is illegal. Criminal copyright infringement, including infringement without monetary gain, is investigated by the FBI and is punishable by up to 5 years in prison and a fine of $250,000.

Chapter 1

"D'you know what happened to Jimmy Dean's car after he died?" my brother asked me. I shook my head.

Jason rearranged himself lazily on his bed, stretched his legs, carefully balanced his *Double Diamond* ashtray on his chest and regarded me slyly through narrowed eyes. Whenever he settled himself like this, I knew it was going to be a long story. I was sitting cross-legged on the floor, looking up at him like a true believer at the feet of his guru. Jason took a lengthy draw on his cigarette and blew a thin stream of smoke in my direction.

"The car became a legend," he said. "It was cursed, jinxed."

Jason rubbed a hand through his greasy black quiff and looked skyward, shaking his head in wonder. Almost as an abstract observation, directed only to himself, he half-whispered:

"Even the fucking car became a legend."

My brother modelled himself on James Dean. He styled his hair exactly like him, let his cigarette hang off his lower lip like him and wore a red Harrington jacket, just like him. He listened to Elvis, Eddie Cochrane, Buddy Holly, Gene Vincent, Little Richard and other 1950's 'rock and rollers'. He wished it could be the 1950s all the time. But it couldn't. It was 1977 and 1977 was not the best time to be a 1950's 'rock and roller'.

Punk Rock had just exploded on the scene, following hard on the glitter-stained heels of Glam Rock and the weird introspection of Prog Rock and it was Punk that was now vying with Disco for the affections of the nation's youth. Other youth cults left my brother alone but I was losing count of the number of fist fights and run-ins Jason (and some of his 'greaser' pals from the motorbike shop he worked in) was having with the Punks in our area. They were pretty bruising encounters – chains, fence posts and bottles had been involved and my brother had calluses on his knuckles and a scar above his right eye to show for it.

The night he'd been cut he was brought home by Darren from the bike shop, having used his white T-shirt to mop up a seemingly endless quantity of blood. The T-shirt was more red than white. Our mother nearly fainted. Later, we all had to get a cab down to casualty. All he said to Mum was: "If you think this is bad, you should see the other bloke."

At the time, the aggro with the Punks had reached such a zenith that the word on the street was that Johnny Rochester (the self-styled 'King Punk' in our area) had put a 'contract' out on our Jason: two hundred quid to any Punk who could put Jace in hospital for a week. However, it had all died down recently – after Johnny Rochester had found himself in custody for stabbing a policeman who'd stopped him on 'sus'.

"Are you listening to me, *dipshit*?" Jason snarled, slinging the ashtray at my head. By some lucky instinct I ducked at the critical moment and the ashtray smashed into the wall above me, scattering a shower of fag butts and powdery ash all over my head.

"You can clean that up later," Jason continued nonchalantly. "I'm trying to *educate* you here. Now, I asked you a frigging question: do you or do you not know the legend of James Dean's car?" He stared at me angrily with hard, insistent azure eyes.

"No," I replied, shifting uncomfortably. "I don't."

"Well, do you *want* to know the legend of James Dean's car?" he asked, in a tone that indicated this was not actually a question.

"Sure," I said as calmly as I could manage. "Okay."

"Well, don't do me any fucking favours, *poof boy*!" Jason sneered. He leaned back against the headboard and clasped his hands behind his head.

"Yes, please, Jace, I'd very much like to know more." I said dutifully, hoping nothing in the cadence of my voice sounded even remotely sarcastic. Over the years, I'd learned the hard way that it was always the safest policy to try to pacify Jason; whether he was joking or angry, deference was always my best ploy. "I'd honestly really like to know." I added as earnestly as I could.

"Okay then," Jason said, satisfied. "Right you are, LB. After the crash, the wreckage of Dean's car – which was called 'Little Bastard' by the way – was bought by this customiser guy for a few thousand bucks. The rules over there were different then so you could legally cannibalise any old crashed vehicle and re-use any of its undamaged parts. Anyway, this guy sold the engine and some other bits to these two doctors who used to race cars in their spare time. One of them put Little Bastard's engine in his car while the other one put Little Bastard's drivetrain into his car. Then they went out racing each other on the track."

Jason paused for effect, inhaling deeply on his cigarette.

"Guess what happened next, LB?" he asked, exhaling a thin trail of smoke in my direction.

"What?" I asked.

"They both crashed," he replied, deadpan. "The doc who had the engine barrelled straight into a tree and died. Blam!"

Jason smacked his hands together suddenly and seemed satisfied when I blinked and jumped.

"Meanwhile," he continued. "The other quack's car – the one with Little Bastard's drivetrain – flipped over and rolled. And it kept on rolling. The guy had some pretty serious injuries; he never walked again."

"Jesus," I said, hoping I sounded sufficiently impressed.

"Here, fetch me back that ashtray, LB," Jason said, cupping his hand below the drooping column of ash on his fag. I stood up and did as I was told, hoping the ashtray wasn't going to be lobbed at my head again. Jason snatched it from me and tipped ash into it with a practised flick of his thumb.

"Sit down," he said. "*Jackanory* ain't over yet!"

Once again, I did as I was told.

"So anyway, after this, two tea leaves broke into the customiser's garage where the rest of the remains of Little Bastard was kept. They were hoping to nick some souvenirs from the wreckage. Well, they failed, didn't they? One of them slipped over and cut himself wide open on a piece of jagged metal sticking out of the steering column."

At this point Jason mimed cutting himself on an imaginary sharp object. He did a silent scream mime and then looked over at me to make sure I was watching. Then he continued.

"The other fucker injured himself trying to pry the driver's seat loose. At this point the customiser got spooked and decided to sell all the remaining wreckage lock, stock and barrel. However, at exactly this point, the California State cops persuaded him to lend the wreckage to them so they could put on some sort of travelling 'road safety' show. The customiser bloke agreed. Then, just before the cops came to pick up the pieces, this young geezer turned up at the customiser's garage with a story to tell."

Jason paused to grind out his cigarette. Mercifully, this time, the ashtray remained beside him on the bed. I was now actually properly interested and I edged forward to hear him better.

"Earlier on, the customiser had sold this kid two of Little Bastard's tyres. The kid told him that *both* tyres had blown out *simultaneously* and with absolutely no prior warning whatsoever. Just like that – *blam blam!* – sending the kid crashing, at full speed, into a ditch."

"Jesus," I said again, this time fully meaning it.

"Exactly," said my brother, feeding off my enthusiasm. "But…it gets even fucking *worse*."

He fumbled for his pack of *No. 6* and lit up another gasper. Once he'd taken the first drag it seemed to fortify him to deliver the remainder of his horrifying story.

"So, the cops came round and picked up the wreck of Little Bastard, seemingly unaware of all the shit that had gone down previously. They still wanted to do their whole 'road safety' campaign thing, using the wreckage of Little Bastard as the centrepiece of their display. Well, the first road safety exhibition went okay and all seemed well enough. They had this whole nationwide tour planned and the idea was to drag this thing all over the United States to promote safer driving. Then, right after that very first display and right when the wreckage of Little Bastard was put into storage to await its next exhibition, the *entire garage* that was housing it burned to the ground in a fire for which there was *no apparent cause*. A complete, total and utter fucking mystery, LB. Every single other vehicle in that garage was charred to an absolute cinder. But not Little Bastard. Little Bastard didn't even have one tiny little bit of paint damage. Not even one single fucking *scratch*."

"God," I exclaimed.

By now I was genuinely riveted. I didn't really know whether I could believe Jason's story or not because, as a family, we didn't tend to believe in ghosts and curses and things like that. And Jason was the least likely of us all to believe in anything you might call supernatural or superstitious. But he really seemed to be taking this story totally seriously which impressed upon me that maybe I should take it seriously too. Jason narrowed his eyes and continued.

"So, anyway, even after all this, they still went ahead with the second road safety exhibition; this time at some High School. And, guess what, while it was there Little Bastard fell off its display and broke a student's leg. Then, when the wreckage was being transported to yet another exhibition it fell off the back of the truck that was carrying it and killed the fucking driver. Killed him stone dead. Then, it fell off the back of not one but two – *two* – more trucks that were transporting it. And then, in 1959, when it went on public display for the very last time, it just *spontaneously collapsed into eleven separate pieces for no apparent reason*! Go figure that one out! And finally, in 1960 – just seventeen years ago, this is – those same eleven broken pieces were loaded onto a truck in Miami to be sent back to Los Angeles. But when the truck arrived in LA and the tailgate was opened – guess what?"

I had no idea. I just stared at Jason blankly, utterly rapt.

"Little Bastard had completely vanished into thin air, right in the middle of the journey; vanished completely. And, to this very day, it has never, ever been seen again. True story, LB."

The coldest of shivers went up my spine. Jason threw himself flat across his bed, apparently exhausted from the sheer effort of telling his tale. Stunned, I sat picking threads in the carpet, trying to commit the details of the story to memory so I could retell it to my school friends.

Suddenly, Jason leapt off the bed, stood over me and pulled me up roughly by the hair. I shrieked and put my hands on top of his hands on top of my head, trying urgently and hopelessly to somehow alleviate the burning pain coursing through my scalp as I scrambled to my feet. Jason had a malevolent smile on his face that scared me even more than his story.

"That fucking car's cursed," Jason sneered in my ear. "Little Bastard is jinxed, cursed. Just like *you*!" Then he opened his bedroom door with one hand while still holding me by the hair with the other. "And *that's* why I call *you* Little Bastard, LB. Because *you're* cursed and you're a fucking jinx too."

The final word of that sentence coincided with his biker's boot smashing into my backside, sending me sprawling, face first, onto the upstairs landing.

"Now, fuck off and do something useful," Jason snarled before slamming his bedroom door.

I lay there prone and motionless until I heard the strains of Gene Vincent's 'Be-Bop-A-Lula' emanating from Jason's stereo; a sure sign he wasn't about to emerge and administer a further swift boot to my body.

I had grown somewhat accustomed to my brother's psychopathic treatment of me over the years. That wasn't to say I understood it or condoned it – it simply reflected that I'd grown *accustomed* to it. I'd learned to *tolerate* it. After all, what else could I do? I was only fourteen whereas he was nineteen, almost twenty. And besides, he was actually my *brother*. And he wasn't *always* like that. There were rare occasions – admittedly getting more rare as I grew older – when he could be okay. However, this only made it harder to predict when he was going to turn psycho on me – which somehow actually made it worse.

Jason never called me by my name, Robin. Instead, he called me "Little Bastard" or, more precisely, he called me "LB" (which he always claimed to our clueless mother stood for 'Little Brother' instead). I think that's another reason why the story of James Dean's car appealed to him so much. The whole 'LB' thing was a weird coincidence he saw as a kind of justification.

It was a paradox for me – he was my brother but I also knew he was a total knob. How does anyone square that circle? Especially when you're smaller and younger and powerless by comparison. Besides, how could I argue with him about anything? He was now officially the 'man of the house' since our dad had walked out on us. My mother relied on him. I relied on him. We *both* relied on him. Besides, I had to keep reminding myself, he wasn't completely horrible all the time. Very, very occasionally he could be nice. Sometimes he'd tell me stories – like the one about James Dean's car. Sometimes he'd even try to "educate" me (as he put it) – showing me how to do stuff (like cook things) and lecturing me on other stuff (like how to chat up women). On rare occasions, he would even lend me his prized stereo and let me play my Bolan and Bowie records on it.

I stood up, dusted myself down and walked quietly back to my own bedroom.

Chapter 2

Red, white and blue bunting. Everywhere. *Everything*. Red, white and blue. The Queen's Silver Jubilee was the biggest thing in the whole of 1977; a national mania and my mother's own personal obsession.

"Come and help me, Robin," Mum called to me from the sitting room. "The street party's tomorrow and I want to get the place decorated and ready."

I was up in my bedroom reading '*The Silmarillion*' and I didn't welcome the intrusion. I put the book face down on the pillow and stomped angrily to the door.

"Can't Jason do it?" I yelled. "I'm busy."

"Busy?" my mother called contemptuously. "Busy doing what?"

"Oh, never mind," I growled, clumping petulantly down the stairs.

My mother was waiting for me at the bottom of the staircase clutching a large cardboard box that was stuffed to capacity with flags, streamers, coloured paper, scissors and unopened packets of 'Jubilee' balloons; each one displaying a grotesquely shrunken image of the Queen's head like a floppy rubber postage stamp.

"Come on misery-guts, it'll be fun," my mother said to me, rattling the box of decorations at me as if attempting to entice a cat with its food bowl. I looked at her pityingly. She had the exact same cobalt blue eyes as my brother.

"Aren't you supposed to be working today, Mum?" I asked.

"I'm taking a half day," she replied brightly. "The salon's been pretty quiet all week as it happens. Just the occasional old lady coming in for an 'OAP special'. Besides, I want to get this place ready for the street party. Now then, come on Robin, enough yammering. Don't just stand there. Make yourself useful. Give me a hand with this little lot." She dumped the box of decorations in my arms. "Bring it into the hallway, lovey. We'll make a start out there."

And, that said, she was off and away, marching purposefully towards the front door. Having handed the box to me, Mum reached into the pocket of her cardie, fished out her pack of cigs and sparked one up.

"Right then," Mum said, shaking the match out. "Start blowing up them balloons. You're bound to have more puff than I do."

"You'd have more 'puff' if you smoked fewer of those things," I replied, still surly at being dragged away from my book.

"Hey, bossy-boots," Mum objected, inhaling deeply. "I'm *your* mother, not the other way round."

I smiled, held a bright blue balloon to my lips and began inflating the Queen's head. It was true, though. I'd always felt protective towards my mother; every bit as much as she had towards me, possibly even more so. She always seemed so fragile and vulnerable, like a china doll. For one thing, she was so very thin; scrawny even. For a professional hairdresser, her long straw-coloured hair always looked wild and unkempt, somehow adding to the aura of helplessness that seemed to surround her. She looked like a hyperactive corn dolly; an extra-manic Alice from *Alice In Wonderland*. Despite Mum's air of fragility, she had a surfeit of nervous energy and a compulsion towards frenetic activity that meant she could barely sit still for even a few seconds. At times she seemed to me just like a small, unruly child.

"We'll have three balloons right there; directly over the door," Mum ordered, gesturing wildly with her cigarette. "A red one, a white one and a blue one. Sort that out, Robin, while I hang up the flags."

Thus commanded, I struggled, like a poorly rehearsed music hall act, in a series of cack-handed attempts to tie knots in the balloons, accidentally letting go and sending them whizzing crazily around the room like farting missiles. Meanwhile, my mother was like a whirling dervish on acid. By the time I'd got three balloons badly *Sellotaped* above the doorframe, there were Union flags and St. George flags hanging all over the place. There were rectangular ones, triangular ones, cloth ones, paper ones. There was even one that may or may not have had a previous life as a tea towel.

"Come on, slowcoach," Mum called as I jumped down from a chair that had helped me complete an especially tricky high-up balloon-hanging act.

"Bring that box of stuff into the lounge and, Robin, please do try and put a bit more puff in the balloons you hang in there. Honestly, those poor wee fellows over the front door look very sorry for themselves."

I picked up the box and trotted after her.

"Tell you what," Mum said brightly. "You blow 'em up and I'll hang 'em. It'll be much quicker that way."

Thus, mother and son began a production line of Jubilee decorations and proved, if only on a small and insignificant scale, that teamwork was way better than division of labour.

"Where's Jason anyway?" I asked, as Mum fiddled about taping a large red balloon onto the main overhead light fitting.

"He's gone to pick up his new girlfriend. Cheryl. Charlene. Charlotte. Oh, what's her name?"

"Cherry," I corrected her, flatly.

"Cherry, yes, that's the one." Mum exclaimed, seizing on the name with such gusto it almost seemed she'd remembered it by herself. "Damn stupid name if you ask me. Fancy calling someone after a bit of fruit!"

"Well, you're called *Rose*!" I laughed.

"Cheeky bloody monkey." Mum chuckled in reply. "You've got an answer for everything, haven't you? Most likely grow up into a bloody politician at this rate. Well, I ain't voting for you!"

"First thing I'll do is make balloons illegal," I replied, passing her yet another of the damned things.

Chapter 3

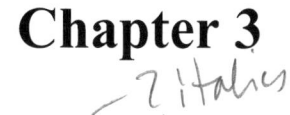

The low 'thrum' and characteristic throbbing of the motorbike engine could be heard from the top of our road. It was Jason on the 'Guzzi'. The big, black *Moto Guzzi* was his pride and joy. Squat, black and powerful like some mythical Satanic beast. And rare too, as he so often told me.

Jason kept the *Guzzi* chained, like Cerberus, in our front garden; tethered to a concrete pillar he'd embedded near the house for the purpose of securing his "beloved". Then he worried about it constantly, twitching the curtain back in his bedroom seemingly every five minutes just to be sure the *Guzzi* still existed. He was totally paranoid about thieves or, more likely, neighbours he suspected might wish to sabotage the *Guzzi* for waking them in the morning (especially on Sundays, when Jason often went out early for a "burn up").

"If anyone so much as *touches* that bike," he'd say.

I ran into Mum's bedroom and peered out from behind the net curtain just as the *Guzzi* mounted the pavement and began its slow, taxi-ing approach to the pillar.

Although Jason's bedroom was at the front of the house, directly above the area of crazy paving on which the bike was parked, our mother's bedroom next door afforded me the perfect angle to watch the dismount. However, it wasn't Jason's dismount that interested me (and for which I watched with a rapidly beating heart and rising, baited breath). No Sir! Rather, it was Cherry. If I was lucky and *if* she was wearing a sufficiently short skirt and *if* she got off the correct side of the bike then I'd be bound to be rewarded with a clear, uninterrupted, mesmerising view of her gusset (and Cherry's gusset was every bit as enticing as those I'd seen in the various porn mags stashed under my brother's bed). Gusset on a *Guzzi*! Jason could admire the *Guzzi* all he liked; I'd much rather admire his girlfriend's gusset.

And, boy oh boy, was I in luck. Today Cherry was wearing a powder blue skirt – about mid-length on the thigh – and, crucially, she was getting off the right side of the bike for me to see it! Wait for it! Wait for it! Go on, love, swing your leg right the way over! Yes, yes, yes – bingo! The *dirty bitch*! Part of the joy – the utter joy and tantalising suspense – of watching Cherry dismount was finding out exactly what colour scanties she had on. Today, Cherry was wearing yellow ones; pale yellow with a sort of white lacy fringe. Oh yes! The *dirty tart*!

As Jason and Cherry made their way towards the house, I rushed out of Mum's bedroom and charged downstairs so I could greet them. I wanted to stand in her presence *knowing* what I knew; having *seen* what I'd just seen. I know what colour they are; oh yes I do!

I stood in the hallway like a one-man reception committee as they entered. Jason walked in first, then Cherry followed close at his heel like a devoted terrier. Mum was pottering about in the kitchen; I could hear the saucepans clattering and cupboard doors banging. Jason glanced distastefully at the decorations that were the result of Mum and my afternoon labours.

"Have we opened a fucking balloon shop or something?" Jason sneered, running his fingers backwards through his quiff, making it even more rampant.

"I heard that!" Mum yelled from the kitchen. "And don't swear. Especially not in front of your girlfriend. Remember, manners maketh man, young man!"

"Fuckin' 'ell," Jason muttered under his breath.

So there she was: Cherry. Blonde hair, back-combed; not a 'beehive' exactly but some sort of retro do nonetheless. Our mother had done it for her for free. Mum liked to do all Jason's girlfriends' hair. It was a chance for her to interrogate them; to find out what designs they had on her first born, to see if they were 'good enough' for her 'darling Jason'. Also, a chance to see if they were pregnant or sensible enough to take precautions. A pregnant Cherry really would put the financial cat among the financial pigeons, not least in our stretched-to-the-limits hand-to-mouth household. A sudden sharp clip around the ear – a proper smack that really stung and echoed around the inside of my head like amplifier feedback – brought me out of my reverie and back to prosaic reality.

"What the fuck are you staring at, *perv-boy*?" Jason demanded, clipping me round the head once more for good measure. "Never seen a real, live woman before? Well, soak it up, sunshine. You can have a good wank in the bog later!"

"Get off me," I yelled, feebly attempting to deflect his large hand with my wildly flailing forearm. I was horribly aware I was turning a deep crimson and feeling very hot in the cheeks and not just because of Jason's slaps.

"Aw, leave him alone, Jace," Cherry wheedled, wrapping her arms around my brother's back. "You were his age once, poor little devil."

I was genuinely touched by her apparent sympathy for me, yet also somewhat aggrieved by the fact she still failed to suppress an amused giggle at my expense.

Mum appeared in the hallway at that exact moment, drying her hands on a tea towel. She was wearing her favourite apron, the one depicting a giant, grinning Cheshire Cat. The inevitable cigarette bounced on her lower lip, making her look like a real-life (but far slimmer) version of *Andy Capp's* missus.

"Hello, Cherry love," Mum gushed. "Cup of tea? I've just put the kettle on."

"Thanks, Mrs B," Cherry replied, wrapping herself even more intricately around Jason and peering out happily from above his right shoulder. At that precise moment she reminded me of a boa constrictor I'd seen the night before on some David Attenborough TV wildlife documentary.

"I'm going to my room," I announced to no-one in particular, seizing the diversion of my mother's appearance as an opportunity to escape.

I ran upstairs, taking them two at a time, kicked the door to my room shut, picked up *The Silmarillion* and launched myself dejectedly onto my bed. Miserable bastard! Dirty bitch! Stuff them *both*!

I read a few more pages in a desultory manner. I read them in that way you can sometimes read – in which you look at every single word and diligently follow the precise sequence of the words and sentences and yet nothing at all actually registers in your brain. Of course, nothing registers because you're actually too busy thinking about something else entirely – in my case, my main distraction was Cherry. Irritated, and knowing full well that, at some point, I'd have to read every single one of those pages all over again, I threw my book on the floor.

After lying on my back in a huff staring vacantly into space for what seemed like a lifetime, I got up and walked over to feed my tropical fish. I lifted the black plastic lid of the tank and gazed at the calming surface of the clear water.

The water was bubbling softly in one corner from the rhythmic effects of the air filter, sending gentle ripples spreading out in hypnotic circles that broke softly against the sides of the tank before dissolving into nothingness. It was pleasantly relaxing – even intoxicating – just to watch that happening.

It was, in my view, way better than any meditation or deep-breathing exercise or all those weird yoga poses that Mum sometimes practised from her Richard Hittleman yoga book.

I could watch that fish tank for hours. If I was ever really angry or properly upset, it was the one thing that could calm me down most of all. I'd sit there watching; watching, watching, watching until all the fear, all the rage, all the hatred, all the humiliation subsided and vanished just like those ripples across the surface of the tank. I'd watched that tank a lot, thanks to Jason.

Originally, I'd wanted a dog rather than a tank of fish. I'd begged Mum desperately and ceaselessly to be allowed one. I wanted something small and feisty with tons of spirit and character; a Yorkshire Terrier or a Jack Russell.

In her defence, Mum stressed the practicalities of the situation: dogs were expensive and we were poor; dogs needed looking after and she was out at work, Jason was out at work and I was out at school; dogs needed walking at all hours of the day and night and no-one in our family wanted to be hide-bound by such a routine; dogs smelled and had bad breath and did their mess all over the place for weeks until they were properly house-trained – and three guesses who would be the one who had to clean all that up.

Mum's list of objections went on and on until I eventually crumpled under their weight. She offered me a cat as a compromise and I gave the proposal some serious reflection. However, I turned it down. Cats got run over or stolen off the streets or otherwise cruelly mistreated. In the previous school holidays there'd been a horrible spate of incidents in our area in which some local kids had taken pot shots at cats with an air gun. Several cats had died and others had horrid disfiguring injuries.

It made me feel completely sick and I just didn't think I could take the daily stress of wondering, when you let your pet out on the streets, whether you were ever going to see it again. So, I turned the cat down, was denied a dog and ended up with a tank full of tropical fish perched on a low trestle table on the far side of my bedroom.

I'd really earned that fish tank. Mum had made me take a fish-keeping book out of the local library and make extensive notes (which I had to show her to prove I'd done it) before she would even countenance giving me any money towards my new hobby. Then, funded by tips from customers at her salon, I was given the cash, bit by bit, to assemble exactly what I needed.

First came the tank, then the electrical equipment, then the plants (both real and plastic), then the sand and rocks, and finally, the actual fish. Now I was in my fourth year of tropical fish-keeping. Whereas Mum had suspected the hobby would be merely a fad, my interest had actually grown and grown. In fact, it had grown so much I now considered myself to be a seasoned 'aquarist'.

I loved those fish. Not in the same way as a cat or dog, of course, but still with the same sense of attachment and wonderment that comes from nurturing and building a relationship with another species entirely; something over which you have ownership and something which feels a sort of loving dependency upon you.

There was one fish in particular – I'd called it 'Mr. Lucas' after my school Maths teacher (a fat angry man with bulbous, staring eyes and an inscrutable, gormless expression) – that would often seem to consciously press itself against the glass of the fish tank and try to commune with me. It would just hover there; all goggle-eyed and mouthing meaningless sentences I had no hope of understanding. In turn, I would talk back to 'Mr. Lucas' – at least, I did so when I was sure Jason was out and my mother was not in earshot. I would tell Mr. Lucas all my troubles and all my concerns, all my hopes and all my dreams and he would neither sneer nor scorn.

It was – quite literally – another world inside that tank; another truth; another reality. It was a genuinely alien environment. I couldn't breathe underwater like the fish could but the fish couldn't breathe out of water like I could. Theirs was a world of order and safety and calm serenity – mine was an environment of chaos, danger and frantic flux. They had pebbles and plants and colour and beauty and tranquillity. I had concrete and greyness and drabness and boredom punctuated only by the bullying ways of my brother and other bullies at my school. Plus, I also had my worries about Mum and her health because of her excessive smoking. The short and simple lives of the fish were clearly far better lives than mine.

I'd figured it all out. The lives of the fish were better than mine precisely because of what they did *not* know rather than what they *did* know. That's because they didn't know about anything that existed (or could exist) *outside* of that tank. They didn't know about their father walking out on them before they were even two years old; they didn't know what it felt like to be kicked and punched and called "weirdo" or "freak" every day at school; they didn't know what it was like for their own brother – their own flesh and blood brother – to treat them like dirt and call them "Little Bastard" all the time. They didn't know what *any* of *that* felt like. Safely cocooned in the temperature-controlled sanctuary of the fish tank, theirs was a perfect world; a world of ignorant bliss. Maybe my life would have been better as a guppy!

I took a pinch of fish food and crumbled some flakes onto the surface of the water. In response, there was an immediate rush as several of the tank's occupants – a gathering of small silver daggers – shot upwards to claim the floating treasure. I smiled as the tetras bobbed just below the surface like inverted vacuum cleaners, hoovering up the sustenance that had, to them, been miraculously provided from the heavens above; floating manna. My attention was then distracted by the unmistakable smell of bacon fat frying downstairs. I suddenly realised I was hungry too.

Chapter 4

When I entered the kitchen I saw Cherry seated at the table. Three empty teacups stood abandoned on their saucers in front of her and she was toying idly with the *HP* sauce bottle.

Jason was at the stove, jiggling a pan back and forth over the flames of the gas hob. Several rashers of bacon were popping, hissing and jumping in the pan. Jason turned and looked at me as I walked in. He had a curious half-smile on his face. I hated that expression as it was completely unpredictable.

Sometimes, on rare occasions, it meant exactly what it said – a pleasant, relaxed welcome (even if things never did remain that way for very long). Other times, it only heralded some new insult or torment – serving as deceptive camouflage; a baited trap to give me a false sense of ease.

"Where's Mum?" I asked warily, noting her absence.

"In the garden," Jason replied flatly, returning his attention to the crackling bacon rashers.

"What's she doing?" I asked, still hovering nervously by the door.

"Gar-de-ning," Jason said in an elongated drawl. He said it in the sort of tone you use to imply that the person you are addressing is incredibly thick. "What else do you think she's doing in the garden, you fucking mongoloid?"

Cherry laughed – involuntarily and rather too loudly. Jason must have sensed our mutual discomfort as he suddenly cracked a genuine smile.

"Come on in, LB. Grab yourself a pew and I'll show you how to make the perfect bacon sarnie."

I sat at the table opposite Cherry and studiously avoided eye contact, in case she could somehow read my mind – in which case I'd surely blush. Peripheral vision told me she'd ceased to toy with the *HP* bottle and had now begun to play with the sugar basin instead. She was carefully balancing the sugar cubes one on top of another to form some sort of miniature sculpture, like a fort. I now focused my full attention on Jason, who had walked over to the fridge.

"First you take some bacon," he announced, holding up a floppy polythene packet marked *'Danish'*. "Make sure it's streaky and *un*smoked. Don't use back bacon – it won't crisp up properly."

Jason peeled the packet open on the kitchen counter and began poking at the newly opened rashers with some scissors.

"Next, trim off the rind. Don't throw it away, though. If you bung the rind under the grill you get a cross between crackling and scratchings."

He held up a couple of trimmed rashers and brandished them at me with slick, greasy fingers. "Yum fucking yum, eh, LB?"

I nodded meekly.

Satisfied, Jason dropped the new rashers into the pan alongside those already cooking, then leapt back as the hot fat spat up at him in protest.

"You don't want too much fat in the pan," Jason counselled. "Just a few drops. The bacon will cook in its own fat. Now, while it's frying, you can prepare the bread."

"Bloody 'ell, Jace," Cherry suddenly interjected. "Who do you think you are – Fanny bleedin' Craddock?"

She knocked her sugar sculpture over and began building a new one. Jason eyed her with a lop-sided grin.

"There's only one 'fanny' I'm interested in, doll," he cackled. Cherry tut-tutted and rummaged in the sugar basin for more cubes.

"Now then," Jason resumed, waving the butter knife in my direction. "Are you listening to me? This is for your educational benefit, you know."

I nodded enthusiastically. By now I was genuinely interested in his supposedly unique 'method' – as well as ravenously hungry.

"OK," Jason said. "You take some white bread." He opened the bread bin and pulled out a packet of Medium Cut *Mother's Pride*. "Make sure it's good, decent, English, Christian white bread – none of your Paki brown shite," he continued, still waving the knife in my direction.

"Oh, for God's sake," Cherry groaned.

"Zen some butter," Jason announced in a fake French accent, whipping the lid off the butter dish as though he were a waiter at *The Ritz* dexterously removing the cloche from a silver salver. "Spread the butter on thickly," he said, doing just that. "You don't have to be a Jew about it."

"Give it a rest, will you?" said Cherry, angrily this time, knocking her new sugar sculpture over so that some cubes went flying across the lino. "Can you stop being so racist, please? It's deeply unattractive. Besides, a *Jew* wouldn't be having a *bacon* sandwich, Einstein!"

"OK, OK, Miss Sensitive," Jason counselled, scooping up the stray sugar cubes and throwing them in the pedal bin. "I'll rephrase that: don't be a *Scotsman* about it. That better for you? Now, butter both slices of bread thickly."

He shot Cherry a wide-eyed glance, as if to say 'Happy now?' However, Cherry wasn't looking. She was now using all the sugar to construct an elaborate miniature wall, complete with turrets, which would have been totally brilliant for my *Airfix* soldiers – if I still played with such things, of course. Distracted by her dexterity, I now felt tempted to ignore Jason myself and join in with her construction project – however, I didn't dare.

"Right, the bacon's nearly ready," said Jason, clicking his fingers to regain my full attention. "Now, at this point, most folk would just bung it on the bread and start eating but what I actually do is this. . ."

He slid the grill pan out, transferred the strips of bacon onto it and lit the flame.

"Grilling it will dry the rashers out, make 'em less greasy and crisp 'em up a treat," he smiled, rubbing his hands in anticipation.

"Don't forget to flip 'em over and do the other side and, whatever you do, don't over-do it."

I was practically drooling as he pushed the grill tray back into position a second time.

"Oh, hark at Delia!" Cherry teased. "The Galloping Gourmet!"

"And now," Jason announced, in the dramatic tones of a stage magician. "The bacon is ready!"

He pulled out the grill pan and began transferring the dark, crispy rashers onto the buttery bread.

"Lay them on quickly and carefully," he said. "You want to keep as much heat in them as possible so the butter starts to ooze and melt."

"Sounds foul," Cherry jeered.

Jason laid the rashers symmetrically across the bread – like corpses gathered on a battlefield awaiting mass burial. I did a quick calculation – two plates, two sandwiches. So who was going to miss out? Did Cherry not want one?

"And now," Jason stated even more dramatically than before – the conjurer reaching the apex of his performance. "Ladies and gentlemen, I give you my *secret* ingredient. The unique item that makes my bacon sandwiches superior to any other bacon sandwich available anywhere on our humble planet. I give you that ingredient known only to a very few disciples – passed only by word of mouth down the generations within our clan. Ladies and gentlemen, I give you *Sarson's* malt vinegar!"

And, with that, he whipped the distinctively shaped flask-like *Sarson's* bottle out of the kitchen cupboard and paraded it round the room, alternately holding it aloft like the FA Cup and then clutching it gently to his chest like a lover and beginning a pseudo-waltz around the kitchen with it.

"Sometimes I think your brother is completely insane," Cherry breathed to me confidentially as she placed the last cube on the top of her sugar wall.

"Just three little drops of *Sarson's* directly onto each rasher," Jason intoned solemnly, administering several drops of the watery brown liquid with all the precision of a chemist in a lab.

Then, with a final flourish, he slapped the remaining bread onto the sandwiches and sliced each sandwich cleanly in half with a single swipe of his knife. In one leap, he was over to the table, depositing one plate in front of Cherry while clutching the other one tightly to his chest. As I'd suspected, I got precisely nothing.

"And that, LB," said Jason, between greedy mouthfuls that displayed the food revolving in his face like wet clothes in a tumble dryer, "is how you make the *perfect* bacon sarnie."

He sat back, satisfied, as Cherry lifted the corner of her sandwich and sniffed at it suspiciously.

"But don't forget," Jason suddenly resumed unexpectedly, the food still on spin cycle in his gob. "The secret's in the *Sarson's*. Very few people realise there's nothing better on a bacon sarnie. Most of 'em go for ketchup or mustard or *HP*. Total fucking wankers the lot of 'em! You can't beat *Sarson's*. Remember, you heard it here first!" He took another huge bite and the first half of his sandwich disappeared entirely.

"Can I have some?" I asked plaintively, all too aware of the *Oliver Twist* overtones.

"Make it your fucking self, you lazy little gobshite," Jason snapped, sending me flying off my chair and onto the lino with one well aimed shove of his biker's boot. "I've just shown you how to do it, for fuck's sake!"

"Here, Rob, take half of mine," said Cherry, pushing her plate towards me as I scrambled up from the floor. "Suddenly, I've lost my appetite."

Jason scowled at her and then glared furiously at me as I scooped up half of Cherry's sandwich.

"Thanks," I mumbled furtively. "I think I'll go and eat this in my room," I said hurriedly, a pretext to escape.

"You're too soft-hearted sometimes," I heard Jason say to Cherry as I was closing the door behind me.

"And sometimes you're just a stupid *prick*!" she snapped back defiantly.

"And put all those sugar cubes back before Mum sees them," he continued admonishing her. "Otherwise she'll think you're some kind of mong."

By the time I returned to my room the sandwich was cold and the humiliation I'd endured made it stick in my throat. But, much as I hated to admit it, the sod was absolutely spot on about the *Sarson's*.

Chapter 5

Later, after I'd been hiding out in my room watching my ever-circling fish and trying once again to read my Tolkien book, I heard the sound of music coming from Jason's room; *seduction* music. It was Elvis Presley – "the King" as Jason always called him – singing 'Are You Lonesome Tonight?' I knew this could only mean one thing. Equally, I knew this meant I'd have to try yet again to see everything unfolding for myself.

I crept along the corridor towards Jason's room, carefully avoiding those sections where the floorboards creaked, applying the same single-mindedness and heightened concentration I would have employed had actual landmines been buried beneath the carpeting and invisible tripwires attached to the banisters. As I neared my destination – Jason's bedroom door – I held my breath like an Olympic diver and prayed The King's lilting tones would provide sufficient cover for my machinations.

I'd tried this several times before – with limited success – but I knew that, if conditions were right (that is, if Jason and whichever girl he'd happened to take upstairs were located in just the right part of the room), then the telescopic view afforded to me by the keyhole might just provide me with the glorious opportunity for me to see something *juicy*; something akin to a real-life version of the scenes described in those glossy magazines Jason kept stashed under his bed. I knew it was wrong – perhaps deeply wrong – to be spying on my own brother but the imperative that drove me (some powerful, unspoken, voodoo compulsion) transcended any feelings of guilt or shame and simply could not be resisted. I was almost *possessed* – an automaton; a slave to my raging desires and the maddening curiosity that repeatedly emerged from the ether to taunt and provoke me into actions I'd really rather have had the strength to resist. This was how I felt as I completed my enforced spastic walk along the corridor and finally pressed myself flat against the relative sanctity of the smooth, cold wood of Jason's bedroom door.

With my heart threatening to burst its ribcage and my eyes already popping out of their sockets in anticipation, I crouched down and levelled my right eyeball at the keyhole. The biggest risk was my mother. I knew Jason was otherwise occupied. My mother, however, was wandering freely round the house like a loose cannon while I was exposed on the landing at the top of the stairs with my back to her so that, unless I heard her approach in time, I would be caught red-handed and red-faced.

All she had to do was trot up the stairs or emerge from her bedroom and I would be discovered. And I hadn't yet perfected a cover story. Usually I was quite good at talking my way out of tricky situations; an impromptu fabrication of something that just might be a plausible alternative was a skill I'd often prided myself on, especially at school. But what possible reason could I have for crouching down at my brother's door hoping to see him and Cherry engaged in some sort of congress? And yet, my demons persisted in telling me, this was undoubtedly a risk worth taking. I just had to hope my mother was preoccupied in the kitchen fixing some food or sitting in the front room with her newspaper and cigarette.

A series of images flickered and jumped before my eye in the keyhole-shaped frame through which I was squinting. 'What The Butler Saw' had become 'What The Brother Saw'. And, in this case, What The Brother Saw was this: Cherry seated on the edge of the bed – gloriously, gloriously, within my field of vision. Jason, standing before her, slowly removing his T-shirt and, as he did so, affecting a convincing pastiche of James Dean's iconic crucifixion pose from *Giant*. Now Cherry was kissing him right on the exposed, bare midriff; her pink lips pressing against his naked flesh, her glistening tongue travelling dreamily around the contours of his taut, muscular, washboard stomach as one of his hands gently caressed the back of her head.

I could not believe what I was seeing. I thought I might have a heart attack and I nearly crashed through the door and fell right into the room as I hastily switched eyes and adjusted my position to halt the growing ache in my right knee.

As I swapped eyes I was acutely aware that, excited as I was by the sight of Cherry (and what she was doing), my excitement was tempered by the deep envy I felt for Jason; I could not help but contrast the lithe, strong, tanned, athletic body he sported with my own pallid, second-rate, maggoty version of his perfect masculinity.

Given we were brothers, I wondered whether one (glorious) day I would be exactly like him and would thereby possess the exact same self-confidence that clearly derived from having such an Adonis-like appearance so that I too would be guaranteed a queue of pretty girls willing to kneel down and teasingly lick all around *my* midriff? Was it simply a question of waiting for the passage of time to magically deliver its miraculous effects? Was it simply that?

My left eye was a much better bet for spying. It enabled me to press my forehead closer to the doorframe without being obstructed by the door handle. Thus, I could rid myself of the bulk of the keyhole-shaped frame that surrounded everything I was seeing and feel myself becoming a much closer part of the action; less an observer, more an actual participant.

Cherry had stopped kissing Jason now and had reached down to the hem of her sweater with both hands and was preparing to pull it over her head. Oh my God! She was about to take her TOP OFF! Now I might really get to see something; Cherry naked!

Entire nights of technicolour wet dreams and hours and hours locked in the bog indulging in lascivious daydreams had previously conjured – and refined – this very image in my fevered imagination and now I was about to see it for myself FOR REAL!

Oh my God, Oh my God, Oh my God! The top was rising up!

Now it was over her head, obscuring her face so she was suddenly anonymous; no longer Cherry – just some sort of 'any girl' archetype onto whom I could project all my sexual fantasies and desires, no matter how squalid.

Disappointingly, Cherry was wearing a bra – the same pale yellow colour (with a lace fringe) as the panties I'd seen when she clambered off the *Guzzi*. Come on, honey, take the bra off. Show us your TITS. Come on, sugar doll, get them out. Let's see what you've got. Oh my God, Jason's reached around behind her – he's unclipping the bra himself. Any second now, I am about to see Cherry's actual, real-life TITS. Oh yes, oh yes, there is a God! Thank you, thank you, God. I will never ever forget this! Come on, sugar plum, get those puppies out. Set them free! Show Uncle Robin just what you've got.

"Robin! Robin!"

No, Jesus, no! Christ alive! It was my mother yelling from the foot of the stairs. If she took just three or four steps upwards, my game would be up!

"Robin, dear, where are you?"

Just a couple more seconds, please. PLEASE! Lord, have mercy! But if she just walks up even a couple of steps. Shit, shit, shit, shit, SHIT! I can't concentrate!

"Robin, come down here now, please, will you?"

Fuck, fuck, bugger, fuck! FUCK IT ALL! I sprang to my feet and, in an instant, the longed-for view of Cherry and her glorious golden globes vanished back into my fevered and taunted imagination. Reality was now no longer wondrous and filled with utterly supernatural possibilities for unlimited pleasure – instead, it was once again mundane, oppressive and blandly domestic. Angrily, I leaned over the banisters and affected exactly the type of voice I thought I'd have used if I'd just emerged from my own bedroom after innocently reading my book.

"What? I'm reading."

"Don't you take that tone with me, young man."

Now I could see her face scowling up at me. Whereas before she'd sounded calm, reasonable and friendly, now my own anger seemed to have infected her. She wagged a finger at me demonstratively.

"Get down here at once!"

Dutifully, my wrath at being prevented at the very last nanosecond from seeing Cherry's tits finally dissipating, I trudged resignedly down the stairs. I still felt somewhat surly and resentful as I stood before my mother at the bottom of the stairs while she rummaged clumsily in her handbag. After what seemed an age, she pulled out her tatty old purse, opened it and pressed a couple of crumpled green Pound notes in my palm.

"Go down the shop and get us ten Bensons, will you, love?" The way she said it was more of an order than a question. "And get yourself a *Mars* bar with the change. Not that you deserve it."

I pushed past her silently, scrunching the notes into a small, sweaty, tightly compressed ball in my closed fist. As I passed her, to my surprise, Mum did something she almost never did – she clipped me quite hard around the ear.

"And don't you speak to me in those tones, again," she warned. "I don't know what's got into you these days, I swear I don't."

I reached the front door, turned back and looked at her. In a voice that would melt the hardest of hearts, I said; "I'm sorry, Mum." I meant it too. I shouldn't have snapped at her like that. It wasn't her fault. It was just bad timing. But those TITS! I'd been just moments – mere seconds – away from seeing Cherry's actual real-life tits. I may never get that chance ever again as long as I live.

As I walked down the front path, I turned back and looked up at the closed curtains of Jason's bedroom. He probably had his *entire face* buried in those lovely tits right at that very second. How come *he* got a pleasure like that and I got *nothing*? I felt like kicking the *Guzzi* as I walked past – except I didn't dare. Instead, I headed up the street in the direction of Mr. Ramjit's newsagent's shop, wondering if I'd prefer a *Mars* bar, a *Topic* or a *Marathon*.

Mum sent me to Mr. Ramjit's to get her fags so frequently that he would usually, on seeing me enter the shop, snatch a pack of twenty *B&H* from the shelf behind him and slap them down on the counter with a theatrical flourish like a Pavlov response. Today was no exception.

"Just ten today, please," I corrected him.

He looked genuinely shocked and disappointed. The wide,

toothy grin vanished from his face.

"Your mother, perhaps she is cutting down?" he asked, tentatively, replacing the pack of twenty with an appropriately coffin-like pack of ten. I smiled wistfully.

"And this as well, please," I said, placing a bright red, shiny *Topic* bar on top of the cigarette packet.

"We each of us have our own vices," Mr. Ramjit laughed as he handed me my change.

Mr. Ramjit was much given to making these terse philosophical pronouncements; he was forever trying to give me the benefit of his supposed wisdom – tapping the side of his nose conspiratorially at me and saying things like "It's a wise man who looks after the womenfolk in his life." Most of the time – like today – I didn't have the first clue what on earth he was banging on about so I simply agreed with him out of politeness.

My brother hated Mr. Ramjit and went out of his way to buy his cigarettes elsewhere – which is why it was always me who was dispatched to Mr. Ramjit's to get my mother's fags every time she ran out. In my brother's eyes, Mr. Ramjit was guilty of three cardinal offences: Number One, he was (variously) "a fucking Paki" or "a Paki cunt." Number Two, his shop "smelled of curry." Number Three, when my brother was my age Mr. Ramjit had chased him out of his shop for endlessly thumbing through motorbike magazines and then replacing them, crumpled and dog-eared, on the shelves. To this day, Jason imitates Mr. Ramjit, basing his impersonation on this very incident. Adopting a 'comedy' Indian accent and wagging his finger furiously, he says: "Don't touch that magazine unless you are going to buy it! This is not public library! Now, be bloody getting out of my shop!"

I was thinking about that exact incident – and Jason's endless capacity for bearing grudges – as I walked back from the shop, munching greedily on my *Topic* bar. I was about to turn into our road when I heard the unmistakable roar of the *Guzzi*. The next instant, Jason appeared around the corner with Cherry clinging to his back like a baby marmoset. I waved cheerily at them as they approached. Jason, grinning maniacally beneath his open-faced crash helmet, leant over the side of the bike and, displaying all the skills and athleticism of a stunt rider, flicked an extended V-sign in my face. Cherry, clinging even more tightly to him as he executed this manoeuvre, looked skywards with embarrassment. A quick twist of the throttle and they headed for the horizon.

A delayed sense of anger and humiliation washed over me and I impotently threw the remaining half of my *Topic* in their direction and then regretted it immediately. I'd been enjoying that bar of chocolate. *Topic*-less and thoroughly fed up, I stomped home. At least now I knew Jason was out, I could go into his room and use his stereo to play myself some Bowie or Bolan records at top volume.

Why so many brand names anyway

Chapter 6

It was the day of the street party. 7th June 1977. We were gathered in the front room watching the telly. Mum was in her favourite armchair, smoking. Jason was on the settee, also smoking. Cherry was, by turns, sitting on his knee or sprawling right across him or otherwise draping and disporting herself as the mood took her. I was on the floor, cross-legged.

"Can I have a jam sandwich and a chocolate *Nesquik*, please, Mum?" I asked, twisting my head round to look up at her in my most pleading manner.

"No, you cannot," she replied firmly. "Just watch the telly. The Queen will be on in a minute. Then, after Her Majesty's parade, our street party will begin and there'll be all you can eat and more besides. So, just you hold your horses until then, sonny Jim. Honestly, you're a bloody gannet sometimes. I swear you've got a tapeworm. I'll have to take you to Doctor Wilson for a check-up if this continues."

I turned sulkily back to the TV. Behind me, Cherry and Jason had begun some sort of tickle fight. Cherry's excited girlish laughter and Jason's low teasing growls annoyed me. He simply didn't deserve her. "But I'm hungry *now*," I moaned, picking distractedly at my shoelaces.

"Hush up, will you!" my mother cautioned. "Look, here comes Her Majesty now."

Frustrated and annoyed, I forced myself to focus on the TV screen. The flickering image showed a long column of horses trotting along the red tarmac of some famous Central London street. Garishly attired soldiers bounced around on top of the horses like mounted skittles. Absurdly, their shiny metal helmets trailed long ponytails made from bright red hair, like some sort of extinct bird's plumage.

They looked completely ridiculous and utterly ineffectual. I could never take soldiers who looked like that seriously. To me, they just seemed like a bunch of lead toys from my great-grandfather's childhood that had somehow sprung to life. In my mind, real soldiers belonged solely to World War Two and they were either British Commandos or German Stormtroopers. They said things like "Eat lead, Fritz!" or "For you, Tommy, ze var iss over!" They inhabited the comics I read; things like *Action!* or *Warlord*. Or else they were plastic and manufactured by *Airfix* and you could paint them with enamel paints and then dive-bomb them with marbles and batteries. And even then they were still more 'real' to me than those fancy pantomime fairies on horseback who were escorting the Queen on the telly.

"This is boring." I whined.

"Just shut up, Robin," my mother hissed through her cigarette smoke.

The pantomime procession continued. Eventually the camera panned behind the soldiers and horses to show a carriage. It was an incredible thing; the entire contraption looked as if it had been spray-painted gold or manufactured entirely out of melted down gilt picture frames from the National Gallery.

"What the fuck is she riding in?" Jason burst out laughing.

"Language, Jason," my mother snapped. "I've told you before about your gutter mouth."

"You've got to admit it's a bit over the top, Mrs. B," said Cherry cheerily. "I mean, a solid gold carriage!"

"Turn it up, Robin," said my mother tetchily, nudging me in the direction of the TV set with the toe of her slipper.

I crawled forward irritably, keeping as low as possible to avoid obstructing anyone's view, and quickly twisted the silver volume dial as far as I could to the right. The sound levels shot up, causing the mono speaker in the side of the TV to buzz and thrum unhappily as though it might burst.

"Not too loud, idiot!" my mother yelled.

I twisted the dial right the way back to the left and suddenly total silence reigned.

"Come on, stop pissing about!" Jason threatened.

My mother had taken one of her slippers off and now raised it and seemed all set to stride over and hit me with it. Her cigarette burned furiously between her thin lips. I quickly readjusted the volume to a sensible level.

"And get your fat head out of the way, no-one can see a fucking thing!" Jason continued.

"Do it your bloody selves next time!" I moaned, resuming a cross-legged position at the foot of my mother's chair. Suddenly, the sole of Jason's boot was placed at the side of my head and with a push – rather than a kick for once – I was sent sprawling.

"Cheeky little git!" he cursed.

"Get off me, *thicko*!" I snarled, rubbing the side of my head. It was only in Mum's presence that I ever dared to answer Jason back. In response, Jason stood up and pointedly began rolling up one of the sleeves of his blue denim shirt. It was a lavishly embroidered shirt with a big stencilled picture of Elvis Presley emblazoned on the back.

"Jason! Robin! For God's sake!" shouted our mother. "I'm trying to watch The Queen!"

Jason sat down again and folded his arms moodily. Cherry shifted angrily away from him and moved to the far end of the settee.

". . .and now the Royal party makes its way along The Mall to the delight of the crowd. Shortly Her Majesty will be further enchanting us with a customary appearance on the balcony of Buckingham Palace," droned the commentary. My mother was in raptures.

"It's just like a real-life fairy tale, innit Cherry?" she called across the room.

"Sure is, Mrs. Bellamy," Cherry replied. Even I could tell the tone of Cherry's reply was insincere and designed only to humour my mother and her Royal Family obsession.

"Boring!" I announced again, standing up. "I'm going up to my room."

No-one seemed to be listening to me any more. They were all too engrossed watching the Queen stepping down from her mobile golden pumpkin.

". . .and here is Her Majesty looking resplendent in a matching pink twin-set with pink gloves and a pink handbag, tastefully offset by pearls and a rather charming diamond brooch. . ."

"Ah, don't she look lovely?" sighed my mother.

"Looks like a fucking blancmange!" sneered Jason.

Cherry burst into hysterical peals of laughter and then, presumably to avoid upsetting my mother, buried her head in a cushion and guffawed into that instead.

As I reached the door I had a sudden thought.

"Jace, can I go to your room and play my records there for a bit?"

I knew that ordinarily the reply would be a resounding 'no' but I also realised that Jason now needed to curry favour with Mum to make up for the blancmange remark – so I had half a chance. I could see the frustration on his face before he answered.

"Alright. But don't touch any of my records. And don't wreck that stylus. It cost me a bloody fortune. It was imported direct from Japan, that was."

"And use headphones," Mum called after me. "We don't want your flaming racket spoiling the telly."

I closed the door behind me and left them all to it before practically tripping over my feet in my hurry up the stairs to Jason's bedroom. It was extremely rare for me to be freely granted unfettered access to Jason's room and I was determined to make the most of it. I grabbed a couple of LPs from my own room – David Bowie's *Ziggy Stardust* and *Aladdin Sane* – and then dashed into Jason's room and shut the door.

I approached the precious stereo reverentially as though it were the sacrificial altar of some ancient religion. The turntable lurked enticingly beneath a smoky Perspex lid. It seemed somehow desirous of the vinyl platter I was about to place on its surface.

Right next to the turntable was a crooked metal arm resting

comfortably on its perch and cradling the cartridge containing the "specially crafted and imported diamond-encrusted needle" that Jason had warned me about so vociferously. I was fascinated by it – how could this tiny, fragile, sharp-yet-delicate needlepoint transfer actual sound simply by riding around in a grooved vinyl channel? Above and beyond that, how could the vinyl itself actually contain sound that had been recorded at another time and another place entirely? It was pure aural alchemy; a truly miraculous technology that people just took for granted.

I lifted the Perspex lid carefully. The unmistakable smell of expensive electronics hit my nostrils. It smelled of heat and static and it smelled of promise and freedom.

The sounds that came from this device could transport me to another reality – it allowed me to travel to a place in my head where there was no Jason, no school bullies, no worries about my mother's hacking cough and, best of all, a secret place in my heart in which Cherry was all mine. I could see her clearly in my imagination dancing with utter abandon to Marc Bolan's *Get It On* and beckoning to me with Jason quite forgotten and totally humiliated. I could actually *feel* the sheer joy of this vision running like pure molten liquid in my veins.

I pulled my record from its sleeve and gazed at the sleek black vinyl accented by a circular orange *RCA* label. The cover – David Bowie as *Aladdin Sane*; a gaudy face-painted clown-like version of *Ziggy Stardust* – stared back up at me from the floor, where I'd thrown it. Copying Jason's own ritual, I carefully blew dust from the platter and gently, even lovingly, impaled it on the spike of the turntable.

Then, after crouching down to check it was all perfectly level, I took the small soft brush from its plastic box and methodically caressed the entire disc in a clockwise direction. Satisfied, I switched the lever from 45rpm to 33rpm and pushed the power button.

A row of red LED lights flickered back at me – all systems GO! I picked up the headphones, plugged them into the amplifier and encased my ears in soft, but surprisingly heavy, padded leather-lined cocoons. I powered up the amp and a row of flashing blue lights joined the red LEDs.

Finally, the most important part of the entire ceremony: holding my breath and with all the diligence and concentration of a man defusing a bomb, I raised the arm and lowered the needle onto the spinning platter. I was rewarded with a loud crackle, a hiss, a pop and an extended moment of almost unbearable anticipation. And then it hit me – the opening power chords of *Watch That Man*. I whacked the volume up to full – with no-one to stop me and no-one to complain. At that precise moment, nothing else mattered outside those headphone cups; *nothing*.

Somewhere below me the Queen was speaking to the nation and, my mother firmly believed, directly to the Bellamy household, of her fond memories of her "salad days."

"Salad days?" sniffed Jason. "What the fuck is the old battleaxe rabbiting on about now? Has she turned into a bloody veggie or something?"

I had listened happily to *Aladdin Sane* all the way through and had only just put *Ziggy Stardust* on the turntable when the door to Jason's room burst open. Jason was standing in the doorway, staring at me with an especially mean and disgusted scowl. A flick of his forefinger indicated I should remove the headphones immediately. The plaintive poetry of *Five Years* was replaced by Jason's angry burr.

"Take that gay-boy horseshit off my stereo, LB, and get your sad little arse downstairs, right now. Mum wants you at this party and we're all standing around waiting like spare parts just for you. Come on, you fucking spastic, *MOVE!*"

In a blink, the door slammed shut and Jason vanished. Then, just as quickly, the door opened once again and he strode aggressively back into the room. Almost as an afterthought he marched straight over to me and, now I'd taken the headphones off, grabbed me tightly by the hair and dragged my head steadily down towards the floor. I tried not to squeal but it hurt like hell.

"Get off me, that hurts!" I whined.

"You'd better not have damaged that stylus or I'll show you the true meaning of 'hurt'" he growled.

"It's fine, it's fine," I pleaded. "I've not done anything."

He pulled harder on my hair, dragging me lower.

"You think you're pretty clever sucking up to Mum, LB, but you don't fool me. Not for one second. Remember, I've got my eye on you! Now get a bloody shift on, you ugly little turd!"

And with that he was gone – the evil genie was back in his bottle; until the next time, of course.

I was only grateful he hadn't smashed my records. I stood rubbing my scalp until the throbbing pain subsided. I didn't think any hair had come out but the entire area he'd grabbed felt swollen and oddly numb. Why did he always have to ruin everything? What had I ever done to him? Weren't we flesh and blood? It was sick and unnatural how he behaved. But I couldn't tell Mum – I just couldn't.

I placed my records back in their sleeves, turned the volume on the amp down to zero (as Jason had taught me) before switching it off and then shut down the turntable as well. Finally, I folded the headphone wires in a neat loop and placed them precisely to the right-hand side of the turntable. Jason liked everything to be 'just so'.

Resignedly, I returned my records to my own bedroom and headed downstairs to join the others. In an ideal world they would all have gone to the street party without me and I could have simply stayed in Jason's room listening to my music and leafing through the rather extensive porn mag collection under his bed – happily superimposing Cherry's head onto all those gurning splay-legged Wandas from Croydon, Ginas from Bolton and Tiffanys from Bromley. However, my mother wanted me there. This was the biggest thing that had happened to her all year. By the time I reached the bottom of the staircase they were gathered beside the wide open front door waiting for me. As soon as I appeared they trooped out. My mother yelled back to me.

"Catch us up, Robin. Bring the spare keys from the kitchen and don't forget to lock the door properly."

She just couldn't wait. She was like a little kid getting ready for her fifth birthday party. The last thing I saw before the front door closed was Jason's hand snaking round the corner, flicking a V-sign at me. I flicked one back at the closed door and added a 'wanker' gesture for good measure. Then I went into the kitchen, opened one of the drawers and began rummaging around among all the *Green Shield* stamps, *Sellotape* reels, bits of string, odd shoelaces and other assorted bric-a-brac my mother had hoarded before I finally located the spare set of house keys.

Back in the hallway, I stopped in front of the mirror to check myself over. I'd wanted to make a bit of an impression. I had black drainpipe jeans, my favourite red and blue *Vans* sneakers and a pale blue T-shirt with David Bowie's face on it. I immediately began spiking my hair up – Punk Rock style. As I was a natural blonde, I'd managed to make myself look a bit like Billy Idol. That was no accident. For one thing I knew it would annoy Jason (as he hated Punks) and, for another, I was hoping I might bump into Tracey Teasdale.

Tracey lived three doors down from me and I'd got to know her because her brother went to my school and we sometimes played *Subbuteo* together. I was horribly shy with girls but Tracey always made a point of speaking to me and she even laughed at my jokes (even when they weren't funny – which, I knew, was supposed to be a good sign with girls you fancy). One time she'd told me she was "in love with Billy Idol." That was all the persuasion I'd needed.

I quickly rushed back into the kitchen and rubbed soap on my hands to make my hair spike up even more effectively. Tracey was no Cherry but I knew that, realistically, I had a far better chance with her than I did with Cherry. For one thing, Tracey was my own age and, for another, she'd already snogged me about two weeks previously.

Originally Tracey had been the girlfriend of my best friend from school, Dean. However, Dean had dumped her for Alison Grant – for reasons I will never understand. Tracey had been telling me all about it as we sat on the wall outside her house. Ostensibly she was approaching me to intercede and speak to Dean on her behalf. I was only half listening. I had one eye on the lookout for Jason – who would have teased me mercilessly just for being seen talking to a girl – and I couldn't concentrate anyway because Tracey's proximity made me nervous about saying or doing the wrong thing and looking like a total idiot in front of her. It was all a kind of pleasant agony.

Then, right out of nowhere, and with no apparent recognition of the incongruousness of her announcement, Tracey said to me: "OK, I will snog you now." And then she leant forward and stuck her tongue straight into my mouth. She held my head quite forcefully and ensured I had no escape. It felt odd. Not actively unpleasant but decidedly odd. Her tongue was slippery and kind of salty and, as it continued wriggling about, I thought I could tell (or perhaps I only imagined it) she'd had a *Sherbet Dip* just beforehand. Her eyes were closed and her face had a beatific look about it as she worked away at a task that somehow seemed to have incredible meaning to her. I was tolerating it – mostly out of politeness at first – but the longer I tolerated it the more pleasant it became. I was just getting into it and I'd finally slipped my arms around her and pulled her towards me protectively (like they do in the movies) when suddenly her Dad came storming out of the house.

"Oi, leave her alone, Bellamy, you little bugger!" he yelled at me. "Tracey, get back in the house. Now!"

Tracey reluctantly broke away from me and trotted meekly towards her front door, pausing only to stick her tongue out at her father. ('I've tasted that tongue!' I thought to myself incredulously). Tracey's Dad raised his hand at her but she ducked it artfully and dashed for the sanctuary of the doorway.

"I hate you! You're a fat pig!" she screamed to her Dad from inside the house.

I stood rooted to the spot – every bit as petrified and embarrassed as if I'd actually been naked.

"And as for you," said Mr. Teasdale, pointing directly at me. "You can 'oppit right now. Go on, sod off. Leave my daughter alone. We get enough trouble round here from that bloody brother of yours."

I sauntered home without replying and not quite knowing whether I should be skulking or walking ten feet tall. Later, I couldn't stop myself telling my mother what had happened. Jason, eavesdropping, laughed like a drain.

"Old Fucker Teasdale said *that* about *me*?" he cackled.

"Priceless. Absolutely fucking priceless."

Some time later a line of graffiti appeared on the side of the Teasdale house. As an end-of-terrace house, it was visible to the entire street. It referred to Mrs. Teasdale, who was about 15 years younger than her husband and who was, everyone in the street concurred, really quite a 'looker'. That's where Tracey had got her good looks from too, I'd supposed. Mrs. Teasdale ran a dance studio in Hampton Hill where she taught people disco dancing in the evenings and ballroom dancing during the daytime. Apparently she'd won medals for dancing and even appeared on TV – in an item on *Blue Peter* no less – demonstrating her ballet skills. Like Tracey, she was trim and slim and brunette and pretty. No-one could understand what she was doing with a miserable old sod like Mr. Teasdale.

"Out of work, beer gut and she's still with him," Jason sneered. "It don't make any sense."

And then one night the graffiti appeared, in thick white industrial paint. It read: 'PLEASE LET ME FUCK YOUR MISSUS'. Schoolchildren regularly gathered to point and titter and mothers covered the eyes of those in pushchairs as they passed. An incandescent Mr. Teasdale spent hours scrubbing away furiously at it with a bucketful of assorted chemicals and a large stiff-bristled garden broom until the offending sentence was smeared and smudged enough to be obliterated. For some reason Jason got the blame.

"Nah," said Jason with a wink. "Couldn't have been me. I'd *never* have said 'please'!"

I checked myself one more time in the mirror and stepped into the street: it was party time!

Chapter 7

By the time I arrived, the party was in full swing. Everywhere I looked people guzzled drinks, scoffed food; gorged themselves stupid. There was chatting, laughing, dancing, singing all over the place. It was a scene of happy chaos.

The sun shone like a laser beam on the entire spectacle. It was so hot I could feel the skin on my forearms heating up as if I'd placed them directly under the grill in my mother's kitchen. I immediately regretted wearing my black jeans and wished I owned a pair of sunglasses. I squinted against the sun and held my palm flat above my eyes like a visor as I scanned the crowd, searching, with a rising sense of panic, for my mother's table.

Red, white and blue triangular pennants had been strung across the street from lamppost to lamppost. They fluttered gently in the breeze, making a weirdly plastic kind of slapping sound. The hum of conversation from the trestle tables sounded like an entire swarm of the wasps and bees that, in any case, really were hovering irritatingly around the tops of the fizzy drink bottles and floating above the plates of jam sandwiches.

I screwed my eyes up even more and looked harder. I couldn't see them anywhere – my mother, Jason, Cherry; they were invisible. I began to walk the length of the pavement directly behind the tables, scanning the crowds like a policeman monitoring a bunch of protestors. The tables seemed to go on forever, like corridors in a dream. Every single house in the street had chipped in to the kitty organised by Mr. Teasdale who'd arranged all the food, drink and decorations as well as the delivery of the tables and benches. A flat-bed truck had brought the furniture at the crack of dawn, waking all but the heaviest sleepers. Early that morning every kid in the street had been press-ganged into a bleary-eyed Lilliputian workforce to help Mr. Teasdale set things up. Jason had personally delivered me to Mr. Teasdale before breakfast. He pushed me forwards, almost sending me flying into Mr. Teasdale with a crash. The older man looked down his nose at me with some disdain. It was clear he still eyed me with suspicion ever since that kissing incident with his daughter.

"Make yourself useful, LB," Jason warned. "See he does his bit, eh Bill?"

Mr. Teasdale grunted and eyed Jason with even more suspicion than he had directed towards me. Jason dropped his cigarette butt on the ground and mashed it with his boot.

"Cheerio then," Jason said with a cocky grin.

Then he was gone; straight back inside our house for a smashing 'full works' cooked breakfast while I slaved away outside. It seemed to me that life was just not fair; some people do all the work while others sit around with their feet up, laughing.

I was still contemplating the unfairness of it all when my mother's voice brought me straight back to the present day:

"Yoo-hoo! Robin! Over here! Where've you been?"

She was waving a hand at me madly. It was the hand containing her ever-present fag. Ash was flying everywhere. A passing child got some of it on the plate of Battenberg cake he was carrying. I walked over to my mother and climbed onto the bench right beside her. She passed me a paper plate, some plastic cutlery and a plastic cup she'd saved especially for me.

"No more party hats left, I'm afraid, Robin," she said sadly. "All gone."

I waved a hand magnanimously and began setting out my plate and cutlery. Cherry was sitting on the other side of the table, perched on Jason's lap. Jason suddenly leant across the table towards me.

"Had a good wank, did we, LB?" he grinned.

"For pity's sake, Jason." Mum snapped. "Do you have to be so crude all the time? What's got into you these days?"

"Well, why else has he showed up this late?" Jason sneered.

Jason licked suggestively round his lips and slowly mimed wanking gestures at me. Cherry smacked him briskly on the top of the head on my behalf but, I noticed with some annoyance, she still laughed. I ignored them and began scanning the table, wondering what to eat first.

I'd never seen such a lavish spread. Bowls of crisps and peanuts jostled for space with plates of chicken drumsticks, sausage rolls, cured meats, coleslaw, potato salad and chunks of cheese and pineapple on cocktail sticks. There were plates of chocolate mini rolls, Battenberg cake, brightly coloured cup cakes with hundreds and thousands and iced doughnuts.

There were also sandwiches; each one with the crusts removed with surgical precision. The brown ones were cut in halves while the white ones were cut in triangles. The brown ones offered a choice of fish paste, sandwich spread or tinned salmon. The white ones contained cheese and tomato or ham and mustard or peanut butter and strawberry jam. Then there were the biscuits; custard creams, pink wafers, chocolate digestives and jammy dodgers. Most people just grabbed handfuls of everything and piled it all carelessly onto their plate, creating mini-mountains of sweet and savoury debris. I did likewise, scooping up fistfuls of anything and everything within reach.

The next major decision was what to drink. Again, the options were numerous. There was *Coke* and *Pepsi*. Then there were bottles of *Cresta* Cherryade (which Jason held up to Cherry's face, jeering: "Look babe, they've bottled your piss!") and *Corona* Cream Soda. There was *Matteus Rose* and cans of *Colt 45* and *Double Diamond* for the adults. There were also jugs of tap water for the tea-totallers (or, as Jason called them, "the wankers"). I reached for a can of *Double Diamond* until Mum smacked my hand away. Eventually, I ended up with a cup of lukewarm Cream Soda instead.

Once the drink had been sorted, I began shovelling food down my throat like there was no tomorrow.

"Slow down to a gallop, Robin," Mum laughed. "You'll give

yourself indigestion. There's tons here for everyone."

"He's making up for lost time. Greedy little twat!" Jason snorted. "Come on, Chezza, let's dance."

He smoothed back his quiff and turned the collar up on his red windcheater. Cherry jumped up eagerly, bouncing on her toes with impatience. There were few things she liked better than dancing and, if nothing else, Jason was a seriously good dancer. It was that innate confidence he had – so naturally comfortable in his own skin – that made him a complete wizard on the dance floor. Girls always loved that. If you could dance, it was a sure-fire winner with them. I couldn't dance to save my life – all I did was mime air guitar in my bedroom mirror (with the door firmly locked). If I really, really had to do it (e.g. at gun point), I might shuffle from side to side limply as if I was at some lame school disco. However, the moment I felt any eyes upon me, I'd walk straight off the dance floor and sit down.

Jason smacked Cherry playfully on her backside as she got off his lap.

"Come on then, let's see you shaking that pretty arse. See if you can give Old Mr. Jennings from No.79 a heart attack!"

He took her firmly by the hand and they were gone.

Mr. Young from No.62 had parked his ice-cream van on the pavement. It was the only vehicle allowed in the street that day. Somehow they'd rigged up its speaker system to blast music out very loudly. He had *Mud*, *Showaddywaddy* and the *Bay City Rollers* on a loop tape; perfect for Jason and Cherry to show off their jiving skills. I watched them begin their dance.

I turned to look at Mum. She had a serene smile all over her face as she watched the dance. I thought I spotted some new crow's feet in the corners of her eyes. Somehow they seemed to show up more in the sunlight. She inhaled deeply on yet another cigarette and then began coughing, spluttering and hacking uncontrollably. Disturbed, I alternately patted and rubbed her on the back – like a parent with a baby that has the hiccups. She waved me away gently.

"You alright Mum?" I asked, concerned.

"It's nothing, Rob," she croaked between coughs. "Really, it's nothing. Don't you worry yourself, lovey."

She hardly ever called me Rob – almost always preferring Robin. ("It's what you were christened," she'd say. "I hate it when people shorten other people's names. So rude and unnecessary. Rob is bad enough but when people call your brother, Jace. Ugh!") She extinguished her cigarette in the middle of an unwanted iced doughnut on her plate. I knew I had to stop her smoking somehow – but *how*? How can you force someone to stop? Especially an adult? Suddenly, I'd lost my appetite.

Jason and Cherry returned from their dance and sat down opposite me again, lovingly rubbing sweat from each other's brows like a pair of monkeys busily picking nits at London Zoo.

"Lovely dancing you two." Mum said, clapping her hands together quietly like a one-woman audience. "Very entertaining."

"Aw, thank you Mrs. B," Cherry beamed.

I put down my cutlery and pushed my paper plate away from me. I'd dimly become aware of someone calling my name from a few tables down. It seemed to be coming from my right.

"Robin! Robin! Over here!"

I craned my neck to see further down the tables. Suddenly I spotted Moy waving at me. Moy was a black kid who was roughly my age (possibly a year or so younger). Moy's family had come to England from Uganda and they'd settled here permanently – although no-one seemed to know exactly why they'd come here. It was something to do with some war or some local armed conflict or some such thing. Apparently there was lots of that in Africa. There was Moy, his Mum, his Dad and his older sister, Adama.

"Black as the road," whispered our next-door neighbour, Mrs. Cartwright, when Moy and his folks moved in. She'd said it behind her hand to Mum as they'd stood watching the removal van unloading further down our street.

"You don't need to whisper, Mavis," said Mum. "They can't hear you from here. And besides, we should make all people feel equally welcome. It's called a sense of Christian duty."

Mum never actually went to Church – nor did she have a particularly strong belief in God and the Bible – but she certainly believed in standing up for her values and she especially hated hypocrisy. Mrs. Cartwright always went to Church and yet *she* wouldn't give Moy and his family the time of day. Mum knew that quoting Christian duty to Mrs. Cartwright was the best way to catch her out when she was being a hypocrite. Mum was nobody's fool.

"Yes, well…" Mrs. Cartwright had stammered before walking smartly back into her house and closing the door. She'd barely spoken a word to any of us since.

"Go on then," Jason said suddenly, breaking off from an extended smooch with Cherry. "Your little monkey friend is calling you!" Cherry looked at him with clear disgust. "Off you go, LB. Go and join the Planet of the Apes. Plenty of banana and watermelon down that end of the table." Cherry got off his lap and stalked away from him angrily.

"Jason, for God's sake!" cried Mum. "I'll ask you again: what the hell has got into you these days? Everything you say is offensive."

Only Mr. Parkin from No.25 laughed and promptly began making monkey noises at me. Everyone knew he'd voted for the NF because he'd stuck one of their campaign posters in his window at election time. Most people usually gave him a wide berth – only Jason seemed not to mind him. Mr. Parkin clapped Jason playfully on the back while continuing to make monkey noises in my direction. I ignored him and gave Moy the thumbs up.

"Jason, you are out of order! Totally out of order!" Mum continued. "And as for you Bob," she said, rounding on Mr. Parkin. "I would have thought you'd know better than to indulge in such vile and childish behaviour at your age."

Jason reached across the table, took a cigarette from Mum's pack and lit it. Then he grinned at her sheepishly before blowing a thin stream of smoke in her direction. Mum snatched her ciggies up angrily, stood up and started to walk away. Then, suddenly, she turned back. Even Jason flinched momentarily and Mr. Parkin immediately stopped pretending to be an ape.

"You're going to lose that girl, Jason, if you carry on like this. You're a fool, do you hear? A fool! Now I'm going after her – something *you* should be doing."

I was distraught. Much as I knew Jason didn't deserve Cherry, I didn't want him to lose her either. If he did, she'd no longer come round to our house. I wouldn't get to see her any more. I couldn't nurture my own hopes, desires and designs any further. It was all too terrible to contemplate. I felt like crying. Almost to distract myself, I stood up to go and see Moy. As I did so, Jason and Mr. Parkin started a new chorus of monkey chants.

"Hi Moy," I said, sitting next to him. "What do you feel like doing then?"

Moy had seemed to lack anyone to play with since he'd moved into our street. Even though I was a bit older than he was I would sometimes hang out with him and play games with him just to keep him company. Sometimes I'd go out riding bicycles with him. It was one of Moy's favourite things.

I didn't really like it much, though, as I would always have to borrow Moy's sister's bicycle since mine had been stolen. I hated Moy's sister's bike. For a start, I found it highly embarrassing to be seen riding a bike that was missing a crossbar. However, what made it truly unbearable was the fact it was painted an especially delicate shade of pink. I would often colour up if anyone spotted me riding it. Jason absolutely loved it when he saw me riding it behind Moy's *Raleigh* Chopper. Laughing like a drain, Jason once called out:

"Hey, poof boy! That is the *perfect* bike for you!"

As Moy was so heavily into bikes he was mesmerised by Jason's *Guzzi*. He would often stand on the kerb giving Jason the thumbs up as he roared past. On some occasions Jason would even respond with a quick wink or even a quick military salute; he never could resist anyone showing a genuine admiration for his beloved bike. Very few things ever made him quite as happy.

It was a different story, however, when Moy tried to touch the *Guzzi* once. Moy was outside our house one time stroking the petrol tank and crouching down to inspect the front brake callipers when Jason spotted him from the window.

"I don't fucking believe it!" Jason said.

Then he was gone in a flash, rushing out of the house – with me running behind him, sensing trouble brewing.

"Oi! You! Monkey fucker!" he shouted. "Hands off! Go on, get your filthy coon mitts off my bike!"

Moy stood up, rooted to the spot in shock, his mouth a perfect 'o'. His eyes darted from side to side in sheer panic.

"Jason! Leave him alone!" I yelled. "He doesn't mean any harm."

Jason turned back and stared at me with a menacing scowl. Fortunately, I'd deflected him long enough to allow Moy to come to his senses and take to his heels and run as quickly as he could straight back to the sanctuary of his own house.

"That's right," Jason shouted after him. "Run you gollywog! Go back up a fucking tree or something."

Then Jason spat on the ground, rolled up his sleeve and started marching purposefully towards me. Now it was my turn to be paralysed by panic. I hesitated, trying to decide whether it was better to run for the house or attempt to dodge past him and leg it down the street. As we all know, hesitation can be fatal and my indecision certainly cost me. In the blink of an eye, Jason was on me, grabbing me by the ear and twisting it sharply, pulling me into a painful crouching position. Then he dragged me, by the ear, to the side of the house and pinned me up against the wall. He pressed my head against the wall and I felt the rough brickwork digging in to my scalp. Then his finger was pressed right into my nose as he pinned me by the throat with his other hand. He leaned in towards me, eyeball to eyeball.

"Just you keep that little coon chum of yours off my bike, LB. Or, next time, he gets it – and you too!"

The moment he let me go I began brushing myself down. All of a sudden, he gave me a sharp backhander right across my face. I wasn't expecting it so I was sent sprawling to the ground, grazing my palms on the concrete surface. I waited for the boot in the guts but thankfully that didn't follow. Instead, he grunted contemptuously and marched back indoors, ostentatiously turning the key in the lock while giving me the evil eye.

Having rushed out in haste and, lacking any spare key, I was locked out. I tried pleading through the letter box to be allowed back in but Jason simply went into the kitchen and made himself a cup of tea. He left the kitchen door open so I could see him pottering about, deliberately ignoring me. Once he was done, he came towards the front door carrying his tea in a mug, flicked a V-sign at me and vanished up the stairs to his room. I let the letterbox snap back into place. A short while later Jason's bedroom window opened slightly and I heard the sound of Gene Vincent coming from his stereo. I knew then I'd be locked out until Mum came home from work.

"How about skateboards?" Moy asked cheerfully.

Once again, I was dragged back from a memory to the present moment. Moy's teeth flashed at me like tombstones as he smiled broadly.

"Eh?" I said. "Sorry, I was miles away."

"Skateboards." Moy repeated. "Do you want to play on skateboards?"

Skateboarding was rapidly overtaking cycling in Moy's affections. He was becoming obsessed by it and he was pretty darn good at it too. He knew all the brands of the boards and other equipment and he could do all the tricks: 180s, 360s, flips, tic-tac, up kerbs, down kerbs. He even knew the names of all the American skateboarding heroes – Stacy Peralta, 'Mad' Mark Baker and so on. Moy's father bought him imported US skateboard magazines and Moy poured through them avidly, picking up quirky American phrases as a result. "Radical, man!" he'd often comically exclaim about anything he thought was good.

"I have a new board." Moy continued. "*G&S Fibreflex*, *Tracker* trucks, red *Kryptonics*."

I was still staring at his teeth as he spoke to me. It amazed me that such a small boy could have seemingly full-sized adult teeth in his child's head. I would often find myself staring at his teeth as he spoke but either he didn't notice or he was too polite to make an issue of it.

"Skateboards, Robin. Yes? We can play?" Moy continued.

Out of the corner of my eye I had suddenly spotted Tracey Teasdale. She was dancing on her own by the ice cream van. She was wearing a pink dress with a white lace collar and cuffs. Her long dark hair cascaded down her back and flew around with a life of its own. She had her eyes tightly shut and seemed to be in a world of her own, dancing freely. Her arms waved this way and that, her body twisting and swaying, her feet stomping and sliding. She looked beautiful. I remembered the kiss. Emboldened, I decided to approach her.

"Sorry Moy," I said. "There's something I have to do. I'll be right back, I promise."

So saying, I was up and gone, snaking through the crowd as stealthily as I could manage, creeping up on Tracey, hoping to make a grand and dramatic entrance. I loved watching girls dance. They were always naturally so good at it, unlike most of us boys. I'd never yet seen a girl who couldn't dance. Boys who could dance were as rare as hen's teeth – Jason being the one example I could name. Cherry was brilliant at it – but Tracey wasn't bad either. For a moment I just stood there watching as Tracey continued swaying and bopping, wholly oblivious of my presence. She'd put on some of her mother's make-up. Blue eye shadow, mascara and bright red lipstick looked a bit out of place on a fourteen year old girl and I had to do a quick double-take to be sure it really was her.

When the song finished and the dancers were either applauding or dispersing before the next song, I made my move. I stepped forward and tapped Tracey on the shoulder. She spun round with a beaming smile. However, her smile evaporated the very instant she saw it was me who'd touched her. I hadn't expected that reaction and it both horrified and totally threw me.

"Oh, it's you," said Tracey flatly.

"Were you expecting someone else?" I asked

Tracey said nothing. Mr. Young had grabbed the microphone in the ice cream van and was loudly announcing a change in the music. His precise words didn't register but I caught something about "bear with me, folks" and "…one for the Mums and Dads out there."

"What d'you want, Robin?" Tracey asked, hands planted firmly on hips. Her tone was not at all friendly. What exactly had I done? That kiss was only two weeks ago. What on earth could have changed in that time?

"Er… um … " I stammered.

"Come on, I haven't got all day!" she snapped.

"Er… do you want to come down to the park with me?" I spluttered. "We could…er … have some fun." I tried to be as suggestive as possible. I also coloured up; rapidly turning an especially maroon shade of beetroot.

Tracey started laughing. Then she stepped towards me and pushed me in the chest. It was so unexpected I stumbled backwards and fell on the ground. As I fell, I reached out and grabbed a middle-aged woman's dress. She spun round in shock and promptly threw a glass of orange juice all over my T-shirt. Everyone laughed uproariously at my *Keystone Kops* antics. Tracey stood over me briefly.

"You had your chance. I'm with Paul Robinson now."

Then she was gone, melting away into the crowd while leaving me lying on the ground among a grotesque assembly of cackling onlookers. An elderly man I'd never seen before helped me up. His bulbous eyes were washed out and watery grey and his face looked as though it were made of dirty chamois leather. He looked gruff but his manner was kindly.

"Women, eh, son?" he whispered to me confidentially. "Can't live with 'em, can't live without 'em, eh?"

In my haste to escape the scene of my humiliation, I forgot to thank him. I just dusted myself down and ran home, the mocking sound of cruel adult laughter ringing in my ears.

All I could think about as I put the key in the door and rushed upstairs to my room was that I hoped Jason hadn't seen what had happened between Tracey and me. I'd never hear the end of it if he had. He would re-enact it endlessly and, no doubt, he would do it in front of Cherry for double the humiliation.

I threw myself on my bed and buried my face in my pillow. How could Tracey have moved on to Paul Robinson in just two weeks? I got up and locked the bedroom door. Then I fixed a chair under the door handle for good measure before flinging myself back on the bed and burying my face once more. Why couldn't I be more like Jason? Why couldn't I have a proper brother? Why was *my* life always so damn *unfair*?

Chapter 8

We were trying to watch the Wimbledon women's final on TV.

"Wouldn't it be fabulous if a British woman could win Wimbledon in Jubilee year?" Mum said.

She was really excited. Normally she wouldn't have been bothered about the tennis but this year it seemed to be a central part of the whole 'Jubilee' thing and Mum was totally caught up in it. No-one said anything in reply.

"Phew! This is worse than '76," Mum continued, placing the tray of cucumber sandwiches (crusts carefully removed) next to the teapot on the footstool we were using as a makeshift table in front of the sofa.

"It bloody well is not," Jason growled, reaching across for a handful of sandwiches, which he piled one on top of another before shoving two in his gob at the same time. "'76 was far hotter," he announced, the second syllable of 'hotter' sending a spray of crumbs onto the carpet. Mum stood with her hands on her hips, looking at her eldest son as though he were an exhibit in some freak show.

"Jason! Where are your manners? Those sandwiches are for *everybody* – not just you. And besides, it's 'ladies first' as any 'gentleman' knows. You should at least have offered one to Cherry before you dived in."

Jason replied with a long, loud, burp. It was one of those oddly elongated ones that sounds like a kind of groaning – and which Kevin O'Connolly from school sometimes used to speak entire sentences (which he alone found both extremely clever and deeply funny). Mum ignored Jason's burp. She merely shook her head and snatched up the plate of sandwiches.

She had stopped trying to discipline Jason these days. She would never refrain from criticising him and trying to point out 'the error of his ways' but there was nothing she could actually do to him physically any longer (whereas I still got the occasional clip around the ear if I stepped out of line). Mum offered Cherry a sandwich. Cherry took one with a loud and clear 'thank you' that was directed at Jason as much as to our mother.

"Are you hot, Cherry, love?" Mum asked, replacing the plate by the teapot.

"Yeah, I am a bit Mrs. B," Cherry replied, fanning herself with her own hand to prove the point.

"Oh, she's hot alright!" Jason cackled, suddenly shoving one of his hands right up Cherry's short blue pleated skirt.

Caught unawares by Jason's hand suddenly thrusting up between her legs, and thoroughly embarrassed to have been grabbed so intimately in front of my mother and myself, both of Cherry's legs involuntarily shot up in the air. As this happened, one of her feet collided with the underside of the footstool on which the tea and sandwiches had been balanced. The teapot, crockery and sandwiches went flying up into the air. Although I'd been sprawled full length on the floor, I reacted with an agility that surprised even myself.

I rolled towards the melee and made a mid-air diving catch, of which even Gordon Banks would have been proud, clutching one of the cups (fully intact) to my chest before landing back on the floor and rolling away again just like the England 'keeper. Unfortunately, I landed squarely on one of the saucers and snapped it with a loud crack. There was tea all over the carpet, most of the other crockery was broken and there was tea all down the front of my pale blue Marc Bolan t-shirt.

"Jason!" Mum screamed – louder than I thought was possible – before she promptly burst into tears and ran into the kitchen.

Cherry was standing up and still looking highly embarrassed – and angry at Jason at the same time – while I was still clutching the cup and staring at my ruined t-shirt and wondering if the stain would ever wash out. 'Now my t-shirt really is a tea shirt!' I thought to myself but I didn't think it was the right moment to share the joke.

"You stupid *stupid* bastard!" Cherry hissed at Jason under her breath. "What the hell did you do that for?"

"Oh, stop moaning you moody cow!" Jason shrugged. "It was just a joke, that's all. What did you go kicking your legs up in the air like that for anyway? It's not the first time I've grabbed you there is it? Usually, you love it!" He shot her a cheesy grin. Cherry pushed past him.

"I'm going to the kitchen to speak to your mother. If you have any sense at all, you'll come too."

"Oh, she'll get over it," Jason said, with a wave of his hand. "It was an accident. It's not the end of the world, is it?"

Cherry shook her head at him and, with a swish of her short skirt, she was gone. Jason's attention now turned to me. His eyes narrowed. Still clutching the teacup protectively in front of me, I backed away as far as I could. Unfortunately, there was nowhere to go. In two strides, Jason was on me.

"It's all *your* fault, LB" he sneered, aiming a kick at me.

I managed to swerve sufficiently to avoid the kick. Unfortunately, the tip of his boot connected with the teacup I'd saved, tore it from my grasp (leaving me holding only the handle) and sent it crashing (and smashing) into the wall behind me. I couldn't help it but I started laughing hysterically as it smashed. It was sort of comic and tragic at the same time.

Jason had raised the back of his hand to strike me but my sudden and unexpected laughter seemed to stop him in his tracks. Instead, he just showed me his gritted teeth, turned on his heel and headed in the direction of the kitchen. Once he'd gone, I got down on my knees and began the task of cleaning up; first I righted the footstool then I collected all the bits of broken crockery and finally I picked up the carpet-covered pieces of sandwich.

Twenty-or-so minutes later we were all back gathered round the telly in the front room once more. A fresh brew had been made (Cherry did it this time) and on this occasion the tea was served in mugs. There were no more sandwiches but I was allowed a *Penguin* biscuit from the tin. Only green or gold ones were left but I didn't mind. I took a green one and sneakily stuck a gold one in my pocket for later. By the time we reconvened, Virginia Wade had lost the first set. I was on the floor again. I was stretched out on my belly, propping my head on my hands and staring up at the telly.

"Move back, Robin," said Mum. "You'll damage your eyes."

I inched back a token distance. I didn't want to be within easy reach of Jason's boots. He and Cherry were sprawled on the sofa directly behind me. Mum was in her armchair, playing virtually every shot that Ginny Wade hit.

"If just one more drop of tea gets spilled…" she warned.

I tried watching the tennis for a bit. I couldn't really get into it though. It all looked a bit twee and pat-a-cake. These two women skipping around and pinging some little white ball at each other. And then a sudden comment from Jason changed everything.

"Come on then, Frilly Knickers," he whooped. "Give it some!" he shouted as Ginny closed in on a forehand. "Wey-hey! Atta-girl!"

And from that moment onwards, I was distracted. Or, to be precise, from that moment onwards I was utterly *fixated*. I'd twigged that each time the women sat down between games the camera gave you a clear view right up their skirts. It was gusset galore! Now I knew why people watched women's tennis! They weren't the best looking players, these two, especially the opponent (who looked a total gruff old trout). But Ginny was halfway OK and they really were frilly ones she was wearing!

I'd been watching intently for a few momentary flashes of Ginny's frillies for a good while when I casually turned round to see what Jason and Cherry were doing and immediately realised something *even more* spectacular. From my vantage point on the floor, if I turned round just enough, at just the right angle, I actually had a clear view right up between Cherry's legs too! Now I didn't know where to look first! This was a dream come true. An absolute beeline right up Cherry's skirt!

The difficulty was somehow disguising the fact I was staring. I had to get the timing just right – spinning around just long enough to bag an eyeful but not lingering too long to be caught out gawping…

and least of all by Jason. I began adding a comment to my spinning-around act in an effort to disguise my true intentions. "Good shot!" – quick spin. "How did she miss that one?" – subtle twist. This time Cherry had pink ones on. *Bright pink* ones! With a white lace fringe! God in Heaven! I thought my entire head was about to explode!

I was getting agitated. I was soon spending more time spinning round to look up Cherry's skirt than I was actually watching the TV. I couldn't *keep* on doing it. Then again, I couldn't *not* keep doing it. It was totally *magnetic*. It was some kind of primal *voodoo*! I wondered if I was fated to spend the rest of my entire life crawling on my belly for a quick glimpse of gusset. I also wondered if I was fated to spend the rest of my entire life being completely obsessed by that part of a woman's anatomy. I supposed so. There are worse fates, I guess!

"And that's the second set to Britain's Virginia Wade," said the commentator. Mum jumped out of her armchair and did a little dance, punching the air.

I quickly spun around. Cherry was getting off the sofa to join Mum in her little celebration dance. As she did so, I saw *everything*. Folds, creases, outlines…clear and distinct shapes…*everything*. It was all too much. I stood up.

"I'm going to my room," I announced. "This is boring."

No-one was taking any notice of me. While Mum and Cherry were dancing, Jason took the opportunity to reach over and pinch one of Mum's ciggies. He struck a *Swan Vesta* on the heel of his boot and lit the ciggie. Then he flicked the spent match at my head. It hit me on the ear. I didn't care. I just wanted to get upstairs.

Once I got to my room I closed the curtains and propped a chair under the door handle. A poster of The Damned stared back at me. They were all covered in shaving foam and pulling the sort of faces Moy and I sometimes used to pull in the local *Woolworths* passport photo booth for a laugh.

I'd started to get into Punk Rock quite recently. Marc Bolan and The Damned liked each other so I felt The Damned were probably OK. Tony Boyle at school had promised to tape *Never Mind The Bollocks* for me. Of course, I couldn't let Mum hear me playing the

Sex Pistols' version of *God Save The Queen* or she'd go utterly berserk but I liked the idea I would soon possess something illicit and contraband. I told Tony to go ahead and tape it and I'd collect it from him next term.

I checked the chair to ensure it was wedged properly beneath the door handle and would prevent anyone entering suddenly. It was. I leaned across and pressed my ear to the door. I could vaguely hear the TV downstairs – ripples of applause from the Wimbledon crowd. I could also hear Mum coughing. I was safe!

I scurried over to the far corner of the room to where I kept all my board games neatly stacked like a mini-tower. There were loads of them: *Monopoly, Totopoly, Mine A Million, Colditz, Risk, Sorry, Cluedo, Take The Brain, Buckaroo, Mouse Trap, Haunted House, Operation*. A few years ago Jason would even play some of them with me – until he inevitably got angry and threw the board and all the pieces up in the air. For a few years after Dad left it had become a family tradition at Christmas for Mum to ask me to select a board game from my collection and then the three of us would sit in the front room playing it together. That all ended last Christmas though.

"Do something with your family for a change," Mum had snapped at Jason when he'd complained he wanted to go out on the *Guzzi* instead.

"I'm *not* your *husband*!" he'd shouted at her.

Mum sat for a few seconds in shocked silence just looking at him. Even Jason looked worried then. He realised he'd gone too far. Mum stood up slowly. All of a sudden she launched herself at him, hitting him repeatedly – wildly – slapping him down with her right hand until he was on his knees. I was secretly overjoyed and yet I was also horrified at what I was seeing. My mother was disintegrating before my eyes; my family – what was left of it since Dad walked out – was disintegrating. And yet, just the fact Jason was getting a taste of his own medicine for once was truly superb. It was appalling and wonderful at precisely the same time. I was utterly conflicted. After allowing himself to be hit for a while, Jason suddenly seized Mum by the wrists and clambered to his feet.

"You're a fucking mad woman!" he yelled at her. "You need to get a grip, Mum. You're turning into a mental case!"

Their faces were so close their noses were almost touching. I felt physically sick. I hadn't thought the spectacle could get much worse but suddenly it just had. And this was Christmas too! For a split second, I thought Mum was going to spit right in Jason's face – or vice versa. For another split second, I thought he was going to twist her wrists and hurt her the way he sometimes hurt me. The moment seemed to go on forever. Then Jason let Mum go.

"I'm going out," he snarled. "Don't wait up."

We heard the front door slam and the *Guzzi* roar. Mum sat down at the table and burst into tears.

"I'm sorry, Robin," she said. She kept saying it over and over. "Sorry Robin. Sorry Robin."

I didn't know what to do. I just stood there paralysed and useless for a seemingly never-ending moment. Eventually, I put an arm round her shoulder. I sort of draped it around her and left it loosely hanging there. I felt her shoulders shaking. She'd finally stopped saying 'sorry'. Now she was silent; she'd put her fist in her mouth and was biting on it quite hard.

"I'll get you a drink," I said.

I ran to the kitchen and poured her a large tumbler of *Black & White* whisky. I didn't know how much was the right amount. Fearing I'd poured too much, I held the bottle and glass over the sink and tried to tip the murky brown liquid back into the bottle. Half of it went down the plughole and the rest of it washed over my hand. I licked it off. It was foul, rancid stuff: like the paint stripper I used on my *Airfix* kits.

I could understand thirsty people drinking beer but why did anyone drink that acidic brown poison? Mum liked it though. I poured her another one – half the size of the first – then put the bottle back in the cupboard. I wiped the side of the glass with a tea towel and took the drink through to Mum. She was still at the table. She'd mostly regained her composure but her eyes were quite red and she avoided looking at me directly. I didn't want to see her like that either – so we both avoided eye contact as I set the glass down.

"Fetch us a ciggie as well will you, love?" she said.

I ran back to the kitchen and rifled through her handbag. I knew there'd be a pack of *B&H* in there somewhere. I took the fags and lighter back to her and set them down by the whisky. Mum pulled a ciggie out but her hands were shaking too much to light it. I was horrified. I thought about lighting it for her but I didn't want to be seen to be encouraging her smoking. She snatched up the whisky and slugged it back in one go, slamming it down on the table afterwards like a bandit in a saloon bar in a cowboy movie. After that, her hand was as steady as a rock. She lit the cigarette and blew a jet of smoke up at the ceiling. Then she took a longer drag and looked me right in the eyes.

"One day I'll tell you why your father left," she said, smoke streaming from her nostrils like an angry dragon.

I stared at her, feeling beyond wretched. This was not a conversation I wanted to be having – least of all under these freakish circumstances. She held out a hand to me, palm open. I tentatively offered mine. She grasped it, clutched hard and pulled me towards her.

"Oh Robin, you're my little golden boy," she said, giving me a hug so forceful I momentarily forgot how to breathe. Then, just as suddenly, she released me. She smiled and took another deep draw on her fag.

"Tell you what, love," she said brightly. "Run and get the playing cards. I'll teach you how to play Gin Rummy. I think the board games are going to have to wait for another time."

Yet again I ran off on an errand, returning with a pack of Silver Jubilee playing cards – each one depicting the Queen's head in an ornate silver oval surrounded by a navy blue background. Mum took a sharp intake of breath when she saw them.

"No, no!" she shrieked. "Not the good ones, Robin! Get the ones for playing with!"

Back I went again. Normally, I would have been annoyed at being sent back and forth so many times, but that night I just did whatever she asked without any complaints. I returned with a pack of *Texaco* playing cards Jason had been given at the petrol station when he filled up the *Guzzi*.

"You deal," said Mum, grinding out her cigarette. "Seven cards each, face down. Pack in the middle of the table, face down. Top card face up beside it."

I began dealing the cards, fanning them out across the table like I'd seen croupiers doing in James Bond films.

"Don't worry," Mum said. "He'll come back when he's ready. Your brother is a hothead but he'll calm down soon enough."

I didn't have the heart to tell her I didn't *want* him to come back. I really wanted to tell her I actually hoped he'd *never* come back. Instead, I said nothing. I set the pack down and turned over the top card as I'd been instructed.

"Maybe we can all play a board game tomorrow," Mum mumbled, almost to herself.

That was our Christmas, 1976. Somehow I doubted any of us would be playing board games in 1977 either.

Chapter 9

I looked at the neat stack of board games. The one I wanted was *Risk*. It was about two-thirds of the way down the pile. I knelt and extracted the box carefully, twisting it from side to side and pulling at it very slowly to ensure the rest of the stack remained undisturbed. I was in a hurry but I still needed to be careful. I completed the task like an army surgeon in a war zone under gunfire.

Once it was free, I threw the box on my bed and virtually rubbed my hands in anticipation. I prised open the lid as though it were a newly unearthed pirate's chest filled with booty – which, to me, it was. Deep inside the box, beneath the board and the packaging, I'd hidden three pornographic magazines I'd raided from the extensive collection beneath Jason's bed. I'd found if I took only one every other week, he didn't seem to notice. There were loads of them at the garage where he worked.

Dave, the garage owner, had whole boxes of them out the back. I always wanted to stuff one up my jumper when I visited Jason at work but I didn't dare. If Jason – or, even worse, Dave – caught me nicking one, the humiliation (and probable kicking in Jason's case) would be unbearable.

I congratulated myself on the hiding place I'd chosen for the mags in the *Risk* box. If I'd stashed them under my bed or in my sock drawer, Mum would have found them and that would have been even worse than Jason finding them. She always turned a blind eye to *his* mags, though, as he was "of an age." I, on the other hand, would have been doing the washing up, gardening, shopping and other chores for weeks if she'd caught me with porn. The mags themselves had already survived for months in the *Risk* box. No-one would have thought of pulling out the plastic packaging beneath the board – plus I'd made sure the box was sufficiently far down the stack to discourage any snoopers.

I lifted the mags out and spread them on the bed. *Mayfair*. *Knave*. *Men Only*. Each one had a girl on the front. *Mayfair's* cover had a glamorous-looking woman with long, silky brown hair. She was pictured reclining on a wicker chair shaped like a teardrop that was suspended from the ceiling. She'd draped herself so one leg trailed to the floor and the other leg was folded back beneath her. Her white lace dress was almost see-through and a split in the side travelled all the way up her leg so you could almost see her knickers but not quite. The cut of the dress was so low you could see most of her tits but you couldn't actually see the nipples. It was all in soft focus and it was sort of classy.

Knave had a blonde girl on the cover who didn't look much more than nineteen or twenty. Her hair was done up in bunches and she had thick bright blue eye shadow and loads of make-up. You could still see some spots on her face, though, which was a bit off-putting. She was sitting on a bed in what looked like a cheap hotel room and her legs were spread wide apart. All she was wearing was a pair of yellow knickers with blue polka dots and multi-coloured stripy socks that went right up to her knees. She had no bra and she was covering her tits with her arms crossed in that odd way women do. She was smiling at the camera like it was all some sort of naughty joke.

Men Only's cover had a redhead on it. She looked quite an old woman to be posing for that sort of thing. I guessed she'd be about 40 or something. Her hair was up in a beehive and she was dressed in some sort of 1950s gear. (I bet that was what had attracted Jason to the mag in the first place). She was sitting on top of this juke box in what looked like an American diner (but was probably just a *Wimpy* that had been adapted after closing time) and she had this sort of 'ecstasy' expression on her face. The way her legs were arranged as she sat on the juke box meant you could see some of her knickers beneath her candy pink powder ball skirt. The knickers were white and frilly. She was also wearing white suspenders and white fishnet tights. She had a slightly crooked nose and too much lipstick – so she was sort of a bit ugly – but that fact also seemed to make her somehow sort of sexy too. It was hard to explain quite why it worked like that – but it just did.

I looked down at the mags and it occurred to me they increased in strength from left to right. It was like low tar, middle tar, high tar for cigarettes. It was *Knave* I really wanted though. Middle tar. I replaced *Mayfair* and *Men Only* back in the box. With my trousers down by my ankles, I flipped through the pages of *Knave* to the particular vision I wanted. And there she was – in all her glory: 'Sally from Penge'. There was a box with a caption beneath it that read: 'Young Sally, 22, from Penge knows the true value of her assets. "Some lad back home told me I had the best tits he'd ever seen," says our Sal. And he's not wrong – as I'm sure all our readers will agree.'

The photospread showed Sally sitting on a chair with a sheepskin rug draped over it. Her legs were wide apart and all she was wearing was a pair of white knickers with love hearts on them and a pair of red and white striped stockings. She was sucking deeply on one of her fingers and staring – sort of imploringly – into the camera. In the next photo she'd taken the knickers and stockings off completely and sat there with the chair reversed – Christine Keeler style – so you could see she was totally naked but you couldn't actually see properly between her legs. This time she was holding her tits up from underneath – making them look even bigger than they already were and she was sort of flashing them at the camera.

In the next photo the chair was the right way round again and she sat on it full face, legs akimbo. This time you could see absolutely *everything* in glorious technicolour. The hair there was sort of smooth and the area was shaped kind of like a mound and it had a slit running down it. Just looking at it made my dick hard.

Then, in the final photo, she'd put a finger up inside herself and she was pulling herself open and she also had one of those 'ecstasy' faces like they always seem to have in those magazines. The fact her head was turned slightly away from the camera (as though she'd been caught unawares and didn't know anyone was watching) seemed to make my dick even harder. But the thing that really freaked me out about these pictures of 'Sally' was that she looked exactly – and I do mean *exactly* – like Cherry!

It was incredible. She looked so much like Cherry that a small part of me actually thought it *was* Cherry – posing for jazz mags on the side for a bit of pin money. The frisson of that thought was exquisite. However, there was one critical difference. Sally had a tattoo (of a bird – a swallow or something) at the top of her left shoulder but Cherry had no tattoos at all (or at least none I'd ever seen). In fact, Cherry had looked at me pretty oddly one time when I tried to check out her left shoulder as surreptitiously as I could. She even flinched when I pulled at her cardigan to move it aside a bit.

"Sorry, I thought you had a wasp there. I was just trying to swat it," I'd said unconvincingly.

Luckily, Cherry let that incident go without making a fuss or, worse still, telling Jason. Of course, I'd convinced myself it was always possible the tattoo that Sally sported in *Knave* was really just a transfer or a stick-on tattoo and thus it *still* could have been Cherry in disguise after all. It was a long shot, I supposed, but the very idea doubled my excitement and that dog-eared copy of *Knave* was undoubtedly my most treasured possession on the entire planet. I guess that, ultimately, Jason hadn't missed it from under his bed because he had the real thing. No need for paper girlfriends for him.

I only used to bother with the pictures in those magazines (rather than the writing) although sometimes the cartoons could be surprisingly horny. There was a great cartoon in *Penthouse* called 'Wicked Wanda'. Tony Baker had nicked a copy from his Dad and brought it to school once. Wicked Wanda was hot. The stories and letters in the mags were always lame though. I called them "and then she…" stories. They were always about various women who were just going about their normal everyday lives – housewives, waitresses, nurses, teachers, schoolgirls, air hostesses – when suddenly they just transformed into some sort of wild sex Amazons at the mere sight of a dick.

Then the story would launch into this really long description of what the girl or woman would do to the dick (or be done to by the dick) punctuated by "…and then she…". Example: "..and then she…peeled off all her clothes…and then she…reached for my throbbing cock…and then she…licked all round my balls…and then she…and then she…and then she"…and so on. On the whole, I preferred the pictures. But something puzzled me. I couldn't help but suspect there was some small essence in these stories that was fundamentally *true*; some tiny grain of fact hidden deep down inside somewhere. I believed there really must exist some secret word (or sign) that would instantly transform each and every woman from her usual everyday demeanour into some rampant sex goddess happily and uncontrollably leaping all over me. But, annoyingly, as yet, I didn't know what that magic word or special sign actually was. And Jason clearly did. And that very knowledge had brought him Cherry. And it really, *really* bothered me. And, as much as I hated it, if I could only catch him in a rare good mood, I was going to have to ask him the secret of pulling women and turning them into the ones in the "and then she" stories and 'Sally from Penge' photo-spreads.

BAM! BAM! BAM! BAM! BAM!

Shit! Fuck! Christ!

Someone was bashing the bedroom door down! I threw the magazine up in the air and started hopping round in a mad panic, desperately trying to hitch up my pants. The door handle was turning! No, no, no! Oh God, please don't let it be Cherry! Or my mother! The door was being pushed open! I nearly caught my dick in the zipper. Thank God the door held fast against whoever was pushing against it.

"LB! Open this door you little twat!" It was Jason.

Scrabbling in a total frenzy, I stuffed the copy of *Knave* back in the *Risk* box. Half the plastic playing pieces spilled onto the floor as a result. I accidentally trod on some of them and leapt up in the air as the hard plastic dug into the soles of my feet. Ignoring the pain and the tell-tale plastic debris, I hurriedly crammed the lid back on the box and slid it back into the pile of board games about four boxes down.

"Hey LB! Open this door you little cretin. What're you doing anyway? Having a wank?"

He laughed crudely and pushed even harder against the door. The chair I'd propped against it began to creak alarmingly. I raced over and, cursing under my breath, removed the chair. Jason pushed past me and strode into the room. I felt I was the colour of over-ripe beetroot and my face felt like a blast furnace. Jason looked at me with a triumphant grin.

"Good wank was it, LB?" he cackled.

"What do you want?" I asked, more aggressively than I'd usually risk.

"Mum wants you downstairs, dick breath." He swatted me round the side of the head. Merely a playful cuff by his standards. He laughed. "Frilly Knickers has won Wimbledon. Mum's having a celebration. Come on, shift your arse, wank boy!" Another clip round the ear followed and then he was gone; vanished in a flash into the ether like some evil sprite. Maybe this would not be the best time to ask him about pulling women, I decided, closing the bedroom door behind me.

Chapter 10

My mother's euphoria at "Ginny Wade's wonderful Wimbledon win" lasted well into the summer. It was still going strong in August – a time when Jason and I had drifted even further apart on both political and musical lines.

The NF had been getting strong lately and kept organising marches in flashpoint areas. Their supporters appeared with depressing regularity on the TV News with their skinhead haircuts, cut-off jeans, high-top DMs and red braces – a bunch of permanently angry, shouting, seething, scary Neanderthal freaks. Jason watched their worrying rise with unrestrained glee.

"The Front are gonna sort out the coons once and for all," Jason taunted. "Tell that to your little jungle bunny chum, Moy or Boy or Kunte Kinte, or whatever the fuck he's called."

My response to Jason was to send off, via mail order, for an Anti-Nazi League t-shirt and poster. I persuaded Mum – who hated any type of politics ("They only try to divide us when the truth is, we're all just people,") – to sign the cheque for my goods by telling her the ANL was a rock band and I could only get their album by mail order. My package arrived at the end of August. I immediately put the posters up all around my bedroom – with the biggest one set right above the fish tank. The t-shirt was cool. It was all black except for a big yellow circle in the middle containing a red arrow emblazoned with the words 'Ant-Nazi League'.

"You'll get your fucking head kicked in, wearing that," Jason sneered when I appeared at breakfast one morning, proudly sporting my new garment for the first time. I blanked him and sat down at the table.

"You're going home in a fucking ambulance," Jason sang gleefully, jabbing his finger at me as though we were on opposing terraces.

"Piss off, Adolf!" I replied under my breath, emboldened by my new t-shirt.

"What did you just say to me?" Jason snarled, grabbing me by the hair in one hand and brandishing his breakfast knife in the other.

"Jason!" Mum shouted. "If you don't let him go this instant, I swear I'll pour this boiling water all over you." She held up the kettle she had just snatched from the hob. Jason shoved me roughly backwards and slammed the knife down on the table. He stood up suddenly, screeching his chair across the floor.

"I'm going for breakfast at Cherry's," he yelled. "I don't have to put up with this bollocks over there. Don't wait up, will ya?"

Jason slammed the side door and trudged down the alleyway to his beloved bike. We heard the *Guzzi* roar and he was gone. Mum sat down at the table, lit a cigarette and put her head in her hands, the cigarette almost burning her hair.

"I don't know what to do about him, Robin," she wailed. "He's getting worse. Day by day, he's worse and worse."

Mum looked at me imploringly, took a long draw on her fag and blew smoke at the ceiling. She turned back to face me and took my hand in hers.

"I'm sorry. I shouldn't burden you with this. You're just a kid. It's just…I really don't know what to do about him sometimes."

I said nothing but squeezed her hand in a silent show of support. What could I say? I knew what I *wanted* to say – "Just shoot him! Put us all out of our misery!" Trouble is, if I did say that, it would make me as much of a fascist as Jason.

Later that day, after I'd had my tea – one of my favourites (fish fingers, chips and peas) – I was in Jason's room playing records. I had my headphones on so I didn't hear the *Guzzi* parking up – nor did I hear Jason enter his bedroom and tip-toe up behind me. Suddenly the headphones' cord was wrapped around my neck and I was being tilted backwards in my chair. The cord came out of the stereo, sending Bowie's *'Man Who Sold The World'* blaring at full volume while I was being slowly strangled.

"Get that shite off my turntable!" Jason yelled in my ear. "It's clogging up my stylus."

Jason let me go as suddenly as he'd grabbed me. I stood up, choking and coughing, hurriedly unwinding the cord from around my neck. I was sure there was a red mark where he'd been strangling me but I'd have to check in the bathroom mirror later.

Jason sat on the bed, pulled a cigarette from behind his ear and lit it. He surveyed me with an amused grin.

"You look fucking funny being strangled." Jason chuckled.

"I dare say I do," I replied, with prim caution, putting the Bowie album back in its sleeve.

Jason lay full-length on the bed, arms behind his head, legs loosely crossed, cigarette pointing at the ceiling. He seemed in an oddly good mood. It probably derived from more than just strangling me for a cheap laugh but, with Jason, it was pretty hard to tell. His temper could switch in an instant – from fair to psychotic and back again. I don't know how Cherry put up with it – or *why*. Cherry! Perhaps this was actually my chance to ask Jason for his advice about women.

"How are things with Cherry?" I asked, as nonchalantly as I could.

"You what?" Jason chuckled, sitting up, grinning like a maniac. "What's it to you?"

"Mum was wondering," I lied. "After you left this morning. She was wondering…"

"Mum always wonders."

Jason lay back again and took a long drag on his fag.

"Everything's fine, if you must know. More than fine, in fact. That girl sure can give a bloke a night to remember."

This was my chance – it was now or never. Here was an opening to learn just about the one useful thing I could ever hope to learn from Jason. I decided to take my chance.

"Jason…"

"What?"

"How do you...er...how does someone?"

Jason sat up again, looking at me quizzically but not without a degree of detached amusement.

"What? Come on, spit it out, poof boy. I won't bite. Well, maybe..." Cue a throaty chuckle and another pull on his fag.

"How do you do so well with women?" There, I'd said it. I'd asked. Now I was telling myself 'Don't go red, don't go red, don't go red' – saying it silently over and over in my head like a mantra. There was an agonising pause. Jason narrowed his eyes and took another drag on the ciggie. He seemed to be sizing me up. He looked a bit like Clint Eastwood in a Spaghetti Western. A huge grin spread across his face.

"Oh, I see. I get it. A 'birds and bees' chat is what you're angling for, eh? No Dad around so it falls to me make a man of you – if that's actually possible, of course. Well, okay then – you're on. Nothing I don't know about the birds. Surprised you're interested, though, being a *fairy*."

I stood there silently, holding my breath. Was he about to tell me his secrets (and maybe even something juicy about Cherry and her 'night to remember' skills) or was he instead going to cuff me round the ear and kick me up the arse? As always, it was an even bet.

"Right then, LB. I'm feeling charitable. As it's 'help a cripple week', I'll tell you what you want to know – and, frankly, all you'll ever need to know – about the fairer sex. But first of all, you need to go downstairs, fetch me an ashtray and get me a beer from the fridge. Oh, and take that fucking Commie t-shirt off first. I'm not talking to you while you're wearing that thing."

"Cheers Jace," I mumbled, pathetically grateful. I raced to my room, dutifully swapped my ANL t-shirt for one of Marc Bolan, ran downstairs, grabbed a can of *Colt 45* lager, ran back halfway up the stairs, ran back down again to grab the ashtray I'd forgotten and, now completely breathless, ran back up to Jason again. I just hoped he hadn't changed his mind. I burst into his bedroom, panting and wheezing and presented him with his required booty.

"What kept you?" Jason chuckled. It wasn't said with a snarl so he was still in a good-ish mood.

"So, you swapped a Commie t-shirt for one of a fucking poof?" Jason sneered, stubbing his cigarette out in the ashtray I'd provided. He stood up, pulled a mangled fag packet from his back pocket and lit up again. "OK, LB, grab yourself a pew and listen up."

I sat cross-legged on the floor. That was exactly how Jason liked me when he delivered his lectures. The last one he'd given was all about James Dean's car and how it was haunted or cursed or something. I was far more interested in this one – about women (and Cherry in particular).

"OK. Here's how it is. Despite appearances, women are actually pretty straightforward to handle – like the *Guzzi*. You only need to remember one thing and that's this..."

I sat forward, craning my neck in my eagerness to hear the guru's wisdom. Jason noticed my keenness and delayed the next part of his sentence by taking a deep dragon his cig. The pause seemed to last a lifetime.

"...you have to make them feel like they drive you completely crazy with desire and that your desire is a desire just for them and for them alone. Make them feel like they drive you mad with longing day and night, all the time. Tell 'em you can't rest, tell 'em you've got to have them – you've just *got* to. Tell 'em no-one else will do. Tell 'em you can't think of nothing else but them. Tell 'em you're going crazy and you simply can't control yourself when you're around them. Tell 'em all that stuff and I guarantee they'll be putty in your hands. They absolutely love it! Can't get enough of it. If you want proof, take a look at their eager little faces when you tell 'em. But you've got to be convincing though. That's the key. If it sounds like a dumb rehearsed line you're feeding them, well then..."

He lay back, cackled and took another drag on his fag. If he'd seen my face, he'd have noticed total puzzlement. Was it really as simple as that? Without my prompting, however, Jason continued – talking as much to himself as to me.

"Sometimes it's even true, y'know, LB. Sometimes that really is how it is – if you're with the right one, that is. And, let me tell you, those are the best occasions to be honest. But, even if it isn't true, just tell them all that, make them feel like that. They'll be purring like kittens."

He sat up, gave me a wink and blew smoke through his nostrils like a dragon. He seemed momentarily lost in thought, pleased with himself and his summation.

"That's it? That's how it works?" I asked. "Even on Cherry?"

"Yes, that's it." Jason replied, deadpan. "And yes, *especially* Cherry."

I sat in contemplation for a while. Could what Jason had said really be true? Was that *really* all there was to it? Would women *really* fall for all that utter blah? Is that *all* they really wanted to hear? Is that how Dad got Mum before he left us? Would Mum really fall for *that*? Is that *really* how Jason got Cherry?

"That's it?" I asked Jason again, still stunned.

Jason let out a large belch and took a swig of his lager.

"I just said so, didn't I, you cloth eared twat?" he barked. "Now, go on, sod off before I lose my temper."

I stood up silently and left, closing the bedroom door carefully behind me. More questions than answers.

Chapter 11

The next morning I came down to breakfast in my ANL t-shirt again. The school holidays were more than a month old and I didn't really know what I was going to do with myself during what was left. I figured I might go out skateboarding for the day or go into town and spend some money I'd saved on a new pair of *Vans* skateboarding shoes.

The last time I'd tried to buy a pair they'd sold out in my size. I wanted the traditional red and blue ones. They'd had a pair of black and yellow ones in a half size too big and I was sorely tempted by those – just to own a pair of *Vans* before I went back to school – but I managed to resist. Some new stock might have arrived by now, though.

I took my seat at the breakfast table and tipped some cornflakes into a bowl. I was just sprinkling some sugar when the kitchen door opened and Jason walked in. He looked as white as a sheet – shocked and drained. He sat down opposite me with his head in his hands and moaned – a low, guttural moan like a wounded animal. Mum looked round from her vigil by the stove. A fag dangled from her lower lip and the grill flamed brightly behind her.

"Not feeling so well, Jason, love?" Mum asked. "Can you manage a bacon sandwich?"

Jason looked at her incredulously – shooting her a glare as if to imply she was irredeemably thick. Then he looked back at me and stared at me with utter contempt, practically challenging me to speak or move. I did neither. Jason suddenly hit the table with his fist, slamming it down extra hard. The crockery and cutlery jumped. I dropped my spoon and it clattered onto the floor.

"The King is dead!" Jason wailed.

Mum and I looked at each other. Mum walked up to Jason and put a comforting hand on his shoulder.

"But we have a Queen on the throne, dear."

Jason laughed thinly – a high pitched and slightly hysterical laugh, tinged with derision.

"The King. Elvis Presley. The King of Rock and Roll, you idiot! The King is dead. August 16th 1977 – mark this date; never forget it."

Mum looked at me again, dumb-founded. She was torn between a desire to clout Jason for his rudeness and a motherly instinct to put her arm round him to ease his distress. Despite being desperate to laugh at Mum's misunderstanding about the Queen, I said precisely nothing. I knew if I so much as cracked a mere hint of a smile, I would be instantly beaten to a pulp. I picked a few dry cornflakes out of my cereal bowl and chewed them in an attempt to distract myself.

"The King is dead." Jason repeated.

"I heard you the first time." Mum replied, coldly. "Make your own breakfast." Then she strode out of the kitchen.

Mum leaving the room meant trouble for me. I wanted to find an excuse to leave as well but I was on the far side of the table and Jason was directly between me and the door. There was no escape. Jason seemed to sense my rising panic. An amused, malevolent grin spread across his face.

He bent down and picked up the spoon I'd dropped. Then he walked over to the kettle, which was still steaming on the hob after Mum had just boiled it. Jason carried the kettle and spoon over to the sink and carefully poured boiling water all over the spoon before replacing the kettle on the hob. Then he marched directly over to me, seized my right arm, pulled me across the table and pressed the red hot spoon onto my naked forearm.

"Aaaagh, that hurts! Get off, get off!" I yelled, squirming and wriggling as my flesh burned.

Jason laughed at my feeble attempts to extricate myself. Suddenly he hit me over the head with the back of the spoon – like he was cracking open a boiled egg. I heard the sharp metallic smack as the spoon hit the crown of my head. Incredibly, the pain was even worse than that coursing through my arm. It sounded as though he'd split my skull open. I could feel a bump rising instantly.

Jason threw the spoon on the table and walked out of the side door. Once he'd gone, I rushed to the sink and shoved my forearm under the cold tap. As I was rinsing my arm, Jason suddenly reappeared and hammered on the kitchen window, staring in at me. I backed away from the sink in horror, leaving the tap gushing.

"The King is dead!" Jason yelled through the glass. "Dead!"

And, as quickly as he'd appeared, he was gone. I walked back to the sink and turned the tap off.

"Well, I didn't kill him!" I yelled after Jason, half hoping he might hear me. I turned the grill off and tipped the cornflakes, sugar and all, back in the packet. Suddenly I wasn't hungry any more.

I went up to my bedroom and closed the door. I fed the fish, telling them over and over that Jason was a wanker. I no longer felt like going out. I couldn't be bothered to catch the bus into town to get my shoes after that. Also, skateboarding round the streets risked a further possible encounter with Jason. Effectively I was trapped in the house with endless hours stretching aimlessly before me – and a throbbing, painful forearm.

What could I do? I supposed I could get the copy of *Knave* out of its hiding place and spend some time with 'Sally from Penge'? It was briefly tempting but, at that moment, her resemblance to Cherry was actually off-putting rather than exciting as it only provided another (albeit indirect) link to Jason.

Instead, I needed something that had no taint of Jason about it whatsoever. I looked around the room but nothing suggested itself. You can't play board games on your own. Toy soldiers on your own can be alright sometimes but I'd outgrown that. I couldn't be bothered to rig up the *Scalextric* or my train set. Both of those options felt babyish now anyway.

And then I saw it – on top of the highest shelf of my bookcase, balancing precariously on top of a pile of *Asterix* and *Tintin* books: the unopened box of an *Airfix* kit of a *Messerschmidt ME109*. A friend of mum's – Barney the Barber (who owned the men's barber's shop across the road from mum's salon and was someone mum had briefly considered going into business with) – had bought it for me a few Christmases ago and there it had remained; neglected and unwanted – until now.

Most of the time, I'd never had the patience for plastic modelling kits. It was a similar story with jigsaws and chess. Anything that took a long time to complete just bored me. The sole exception was reading. I loved to read and freely immerse myself in the utter escapism it offered. But plastic model-making? Jigsaws? Bollocks to that!

I fetched the box down. The picture on the box showed a *Messerschmidt* emerging from some clouds on a half turn, pursued by a squadron of *Spitfires*. The *Messerschmidt* was a murky green colour and it had a big swastika on its tailgate and two more on the underside of its wings.

Its nose was yellow and it had a decal of shark teeth attached to it that made it look as much like a creature as much as a plane. It looked pretty impressive but part of the reason I'd never built it (apart from not having the patience) was because I'd have actually preferred a British plane – a *Spitfire* or a *Hurricane* – rather than a plane of the enemy. It seemed doubly inappropriate somehow, standing there in my ANL t-shirt, holding a model kit of a Nazi aircraft. However, I didn't want to build the thing anyway. My idea, on spotting it on the bookcase, was altogether very different.

I took the *Airfix* kit over to my desk and sat down. Carefully, I prised off the lid and peered inside. The plastic body of the aircraft was still inside a polythene bag together with the folded set of instructions for its construction. Some loose, unidentifiable bits of plastic clustered at the bottom of the bag. I lifted the polythene bag out and spotted what I was looking for – a small tube of *UHU* glue.

It was a tiny yellow tube – a bit like a toothpaste tube – with a small black cap on top that reminded me of the valve caps on the wheels of my bicycle. *UHU* glue smelt just like bananas and I always thought the colour of the packaging (yellow and black) was supposed to reflect that. There were rumours the manufacturers were under pressure to change the smell because some properly dumb kids actually tried to eat it.

I took the tube of glue from the box and examined it. Some kid at school in the year above had sworn that sniffing it made you see visions and opened up a whole other world no-one knew even existed. He'd been suspended from school for doing it after being caught on school property reportedly 'out of his mind' while carrying a bag of glue. He said what you should do was put some glue in a polythene bag, hold the bag over your face, breathe in a few times and then you'd enter this complete other universe. Finding myself alone after Jason's latest assault, I now felt curious. Another world might suit me very nicely if it allowed me to properly escape from this one.

I opened the polythene bag that contained the *Messerschmidt* kit and tipped all the pieces of plastic back into the box. Then I opened the tube of glue and squeezed what I supposed was a decent amount into the bottom of the empty polythene bag. I could smell the sharp, pungent banana-like aroma the instant I took the cap off the glue. It seemed to permeate the entire bedroom. It was synthetic, chemical, overpowering but not entirely unpleasant. I held the bag aloft and looked at it. The moment of truth – stick my nose in there or not?

I was about to do it when I remembered the school assembly we'd all been forced to attend after the glue-sniffing kid had been suspended. Our Science teacher, Mr Dobkins, had stood in front of the entire school and warned us that "the fashion of glue-sniffing was both stupid and deadly." Kids had died apparently.

Others had gone into comas and never come out of them. Some were vegetables; their brains ruined for all time. A few more were reported to have gone blind. Even worse than this – to my mind – was the warning that sniffing glue would give you acne-style zits and skin rashes, usually in rings and clusters around the nose and mouth. Well, how could I face Cherry again (or any girl, for that matter) if I suddenly found myself transformed into a pizza-faced freak?

I folded the polythene bag up tightly and replaced it, glue included, in the box. Then I returned the box to the bookcase. Jason might have made me unbearably unhappy and I might have been desperate to escape him but this wasn't the answer. I wasn't going to turn inward and punish myself just because *he* was a piece of shite. I wouldn't give him the satisfaction. I wasn't going to risk brain death, actual death, blindness or facial disfigurement for the likes of Jason. I'd just have to find another way to escape.

Chapter 12

September meant a return to school – which meant a return to bog flushing, bullying, playground fights and stressed-out teachers droning on about exams.

If only the summer holidays could last forever. If only I could become an adult more quickly. Whenever I felt like this, I would hear my mother's voice inside my head: "Don't wish your life away, Robin. The days of your childhood are the best days of your life." I guessed she must know what she was talking about but, even so, that statement always sounded decidedly odd. After all, if this was as good as it was ever going to get – bullies at school, Jason at home – well, stop the world right now!

September 16th 1977 fell during my first week back at school after the summer holidays. I'd put on my ANL t-shirt under my school shirt and regulation grey jumper and I was wearing my new *Vans* shoes. I might hate being there but at least I'd look cool. I walked down to breakfast on the morning of Friday 17th September and was surprised to find Jason in the kitchen waiting for me. He was sitting at the kitchen table smoking, drinking tea and reading the newspaper. Reading the newspaper was especially unusual for him – normally Jason never read anything at all apart from motorbike magazines and, even then, I suspect it was only for the photos.

The moment I walked in, Jason leapt up and brandished the newspaper at me. A bold headline proclaimed: 'Marc Bolan Killed In Crash'. Jason danced around me, holding the newspaper by the corners while jiggling it at me like a matador waving a red rag at a bull.

"Your hero's dead!" Jason laughed jubilantly, every bit as pleased as if he'd just seen his team score a cup-winning goal. "Dead, dead, brown bread. Wrapped himself round a tree last night. One less fairy poofter on the planet."

I was in shock. I sat down at the table, ignoring Jason completely. The newspaper appeared in front of my nose as Jason continued to make it dance before my face.

"Read it and weep, LB" he taunted.

I swatted the paper out of his hand and it fell in scattered pieces on the floor. However, the cuff round the head I fully expected never arrived. I turned to find out why and discovered Mum had just walked in.

"What's going on?" Mum asked angrily. "Why is my newspaper all over the floor? Can't you boys stop fighting for even five minutes?"

I stood up and began collecting the scattered sections of newspaper, reassembling the thing as best I could.

"His hero's dead." Jason said, by way of explanation.

"What?" Mum asked, confused.

"Bolan. That Glam Rock woolly woofter. Wrapped himself right round a tree in the early hours. Made the mistake of letting his bird drive. Women drivers, eh?" Jason cackled.

"Don't be so damned disrespectful." Mum snapped at him. "Someone is dead. You don't speak ill of the dead – not in this house. I didn't bring you up that way."

"Dead." Jason repeated to me under his breath.

I said nothing as I handed Mum the crumpled newspaper. I think she caught sight of the tears welling in my eyes.

"Have some sensitivity to others' feelings, for God's sake, Jason." Mum scolded him. "Think how Robin feels. Think how you felt when it was Elvis not so long ago. You sound like a hypocrite and there's not many worse sins than that, my lad."

Jason sat down at the table and extinguished his fag in the ashtray.

"Cut the sermon, will you, Vicar. Listen, can I have the full works this morning? It's gonna be a long day at the garage – we've got a hell of a backlog of bikes to fix. Can you chuck in some beans and black pudding too?"

"I'll see what I can do – but how about a 'please'?" Mum replied, glad to have the morning's commotion apparently over and done with.

"The full works with beans and black pudding, *please*." Jason replied, stretching the 'please' into a sarcastic wheedling sound.

"You don't have to be embarrassed about saying 'please'." Mum cautioned. "Manners cost nothing and manners maketh man. Now, Robin, you've got school. What can I get you?"

"Nothing, thanks." I replied. "I'm not hungry. I'll get a chocolate bar on the way."

"A chocolate bar for breakfast?"

"I'm not hungry."

"He's mourning his fellow faggot." Jason chipped in.

"One more word out of you and you'll be fixing your own breakfast." Mum warned, lighting a cigarette.

I picked up my school bag and walked out. I needed to get as far away from Jason as I possibly could for as long as I possibly could. Suddenly the prospect of a day at school didn't seem quite so bad after all.

Chapter 13

Marc Bolan was dead. Dead and gone and lost completely. I was inconsolable for weeks, walking around under a black cloud, falling behind at school. The reactions from Jason and my mother were predictably different.

"Pull yourself together, you little shithead," said Jason. "You never even met him and you're wandering round like you were married to him. Stop being such a fucking faggot." And then the inevitable clip round the ear would follow.

My mother said: "Do you want to see someone and talk about it? Maybe the doctor can give you some pills?"

"I'll be alright, Mum," I replied. "I'll get over it. It just takes time. I'm still adjusting, I guess."

"For three frigging weeks?" Jason sneered. "You're not right in the head, poof boy."

"I'm going to my room."

Such was my daily routine, week after week. I'd come home from school, have some toast or a sandwich and go to my room to talk to my fish. Mostly, I talked to them about death. What was death? What was the point of it? Why did it even exist? At weekends, I'd roll out of bed late and listless. I'd stay in my room, watching out of the window until I was sure Jason had left. Then I'd feed the fish and talk to them about death again. It became my full-time obsession.

Who invented death? Why do people and animals have to die? There had to be some sense, reason and purpose to it – there *had* to be. It couldn't just be random and meaningless – that didn't make any sense whatsoever.

I'd never really known death. My grandparents – on both sides – had died before I was born. My father walked out on us when I was too small to know much about it. Somehow that was worse than if he'd actually died though. For all I knew, he might still be alive or he might be dead. I wasn't sure I cared that much either way.

My fish had died occasionally. They'd float to the top of the tank and bob sadly on the surface like still, lifeless, rigid, lonely little private islands. Their unseeing eyes stared out at nothing in particular while the surviving fish swam around below the corpses, seemingly oblivious and untroubled.

But that was nature – I was sorry for them and sad for them and it upset me every time a fish died but it was the natural order. It was 'natural causes' as the doctors called it. No-one else had killed them – it just happened. I didn't like it but I could sort of accept it and adjust to it on that basis – 'natural causes'. But Marc Bolan wasn't natural causes because it wasn't old age; it wasn't his time. It was an accident – a freak accident; his car hit a tree. It was bad luck but it wasn't 'natural causes' and thus I could not accept it.

There was a boy at school who'd died. It had happened a couple of years ago. He was about ten or eleven at the time. I didn't really know him that well as he was in the year below me. He had leukaemia or some other type of cancer no-one could spell. He'd lost all his hair and looked wizened and weak so it wasn't that much of a surprise when he didn't come to school for weeks and then, one morning, the Headmaster made an announcement that he'd "sadly died" and "we should all pray for him and his family at this difficult time."

Other than that, death was a total abstract for me until Marc Bolan died. Then it hit me like a freight train – with me tied to the tracks. It was there when I opened my eyes first thing in the morning and it was there in my nightmares when I tried to go to sleep. I suppose Bolan's death made me, in some ways, more aware of my own mortality.

Before that, I had that childish thing of thinking that time went slowly and was infinite and I'd be here forever and my Mum would be here forever and my friends would be here forever and even Jason would be here forever (worse luck!). But Marc Bolan's passing had made me realise that we all die, that time goes quickly, that each day is a journey on the same inescapable road we all have to travel (whether we like it or not).

I didn't know how to react to this realisation – the awareness of finality lurking in the shadows, stalking every single one of us; the ultimate serial killer with a very personal agenda. Even worse than that, Marc Bolan's death magnified, to me, the reality that, every day we exist, we all face the potential for a sudden, undeserved violent end and that there was no escape and no protection from that everyday reality.

So, how do you begin to cope with that knowledge and that realisation? How can you react to the discovery that this is your lot in life? My response was this: I started to dress entirely in black – black jeans, black trainers, black t-shirts (luckily the ANL one was black anyway). I did this for weeks. I was still doing it in mid-November with garish multi-coloured Christmas decorations in the shops and happy advertisements for toys and games on Saturday morning kids' TV (both things that, in the past, would have excited and pleased me). My mother worried about me on so many levels while I worried in return about her (and her mortality) and her hacking cough from her constant smoking.

"Are you going to give up smoking, Mum?" I'd ask her seemingly daily.

"Are you going to give up dressing in black and fixating on death?" she'd counter.

She'd try to broker a deal with me.

"Tell you what, Robin, you give up this morbid obsession and start enjoying life again and I'll give up smoking for as long as I possibly can."

I thought about it. It was a tempting vision but I knew she could no more quit smoking than I could un-think a thought I'd already had.

"You couldn't quit even if you wanted to." I said to her sadly.

She ignored my comment, walked over and hugged me. She

started stroking my hair, comforting me like she did when I was three or four and I'd fallen over and grazed my knee or elbow.

"Robin, life is short and sometimes life is brutal too. It's the same for all of us whoever we are. So, what do we do about that? What we do is try to make the best of every single day and try to make this world the best we can for all the people and animals living in it. We can do – and ask of those around us – no more and no less."

"*Why?*" I whined, eliciting the most talismanic and plaintive cry of childhood. I was surprised to find myself wracked with sudden sobs, crying hopelessly into her shoulder.

"The only answer to 'why' is 'because'." Mum chuckled, holding my head in her hands before kissing me on the forehead. I stared at her in puzzlement and allowed myself to be kissed.

"Ours not to reason why, Robin. Ours not to reason why."

The front door slammed at that precise moment. We both looked at each other guiltily – even though we had nothing to feel guilty about – and laughed simultaneously. At first we laughed quietly – enjoying a shared, secret chuckle – then our shared amusement escalated into mutual belly laughs so violent we were practically holding each other up. Jason burst into the room, cigarette dangling from his lips, smoothing back his James Dean quiff and staring at us as if we ought to be sectioned.

"What the fuck are you two laughing at? You look like a pair of mental rejects."

His complete lack of comprehension only made us laugh more. For me especially, it was a blessed release.

"You wouldn't understand, Jason, love." Mum said, waving him away, between strangled sobs of laughter.

"Too right, I wouldn't." Jason snapped. "Pair of sodding nut jobs. I'm going to my room." And then he was gone.

That was it for me. Suddenly, I had the opportunity to laugh – with total impunity – at Jason himself. And I took my chance to the full – falling back on the settee, wracked with belly laughs, tears streaming, gasping for breath, calming down to strangled hiccupping sobs before starting up again to once more scale the heady heights of hysterical laughter.

Mum sat in a nearby armchair and watched me with a mix of indulgence and concern. She could see this was cathartic for me but she was also concerned my actions were somewhat extreme.

She waited patiently for me to calm myself – which took several attempts. Once my equilibrium had been restored it all felt wonderful. I felt liberated and triumphant – over Jason (significantly) and over death (momentarily). It was just a perfect moment. And then Mum – unaware and with only the best intentions – spoiled it. She reached across and took my hand. Stroking my hand gently, she looked in my eyes and then she said:

"You know, Robin, you and Jason are so very different. You're a thinker and he's a do-er. Just sometimes – only sometimes, mind – you might do well to take just one little page out of your brother's book."

Chapter 14

I heard them talking in the kitchen. I was about to walk in when I heard hushed voices between Mum and Jason. It made me curious so I lingered at the door.

"…but we have to do something, Jason. He can't go on like this. *We* can't go on like this. It's not normal."

"It's a phase, mother."

Jason only ever called her 'mother', rather than 'mum', when he was being condescending – somehow implying she was over-reacting to something or trying to establish he knew better than she did. Normally it angered her but this time she totally ignored it, which meant they had to be discussing something serious.

"I thought he was over it that time you came in and we were laughing. Perhaps I should send him to the doctor."

"You mean a head shrink?"

"No, the normal doctor. He's not mad, he's depressed. Maybe the doctor can give him some pills or something."

So it was me they were discussing!

"They aren't going to prescribe anti-depressants to a kid, mother. For God's sake."

There it was again – the use of 'mother' in a patronising way. And still she didn't react.

"Well, this whole death obsession. It's not right and it needs to stop. He's just a young boy. He shouldn't be thinking about death all the time."

Silence from Jason. I could just about hear his lighter being flicked as he lit a cigarette. Gradually the smoke drifted my way and threatened to make me cough. I put my hand over my mouth and tried to breathe solely through my nose for fear of betraying my presence. Mum continued talking, as if to herself.

"There has to be a solution. I just want Robin back the way he was. I mean, you were pretty upset when Elvis died." I heard Jason grunting his assent. "But you weren't in mourning for *weeks*. I know Robin liked Marc Bolan but…"

"…so, do you want *me* to talk to him?"

Mum stifled a contemptuous laugh.

"No. No, thank you. But, you know…"

Suddenly I really needed to cough and jumped hurriedly away from the door, stifling the need by hacking silently into my sleeve. By the time I returned to my listening post I only caught the tail end of Mum's idea.

"…so, if you could ask Cherry to do that for me, I'd be truly grateful, Jason lovey."

Cherry?! Were they going to ask Cherry to talk to me?! It seemed an odd idea but I was definitely okay with it. Any chance of me spending some time alone with Cherry was a dream come true. I just hoped I'd put two and two together correctly and that really was Mum's plan. If so, I'd need to put on a bit of a show so she got Cherry round to see me sooner rather than later. I walked boldly into the kitchen as if I'd only just come downstairs.

"You alright, love?" Mum asked. "What do you want for breakfast?"

"Nothing, thanks. I'm not hungry. What's the point in eating when we're all going to die anyway? I'm going back to my room."

I turned on my heel and left before Jason or my mother could respond.

Back in my room, I wondered if I'd overdone it. A whole Saturday afternoon now stretched before me and I'd had no breakfast. In truth, I'd been ready to quit the whole 'dressing in black' routine anyway. Even I felt it had grown stale.

It wasn't going to bring Marc Bolan back and weeks of my own life had been needlessly ticking away while all I'd really achieved was only to make Mum feel worried and miserable. For too long now, my weekends had just become hours of seemingly unending self-imposed solitude.

Moy and my other friends had long since stopped knocking on the door to ask if I was coming out; one too many refusals, I guess. And thus I'd isolated myself. Only this time, I'd done myself out of any breakfast into the bargain. Still, it would all be worth it if Cherry came round for our 'chat' sometime soon.

I sat down, put on my headphones and switched on the cassette I'd taped of T Rex. Once Jason had driven off on the *Guzzi* and Mum had gone shopping, I'd go downstairs and fix myself a cheese sandwich.

Much later there was a knock at my bedroom door. A female voice called out and, tellingly, it wasn't my mother.

"Robin? Can I come in?"

Cherry! Yes, oh yes! I put on a croaky, depressed voice and called out as weakly as I could manage while still ensuring she could definitely hear me.

"Yes, please come in."

The door opened slowly and Cherry's head appeared, peering cautiously round to see if I was decent. For a split second I didn't recognise her as she'd changed her hair or, to be precise, Mum had changed it for her at the salon. The beehive had gone.

Now her hair was long and loose; silky blonde curls flowing down to her shoulders in enticing waves. It wasn't back-combed any more but it was still puffed up, bouncy and fluffy. It looked so soft and luxurious it made me want to touch it; to run my fingers through it and grab big handfuls of it. It was all I could do to restrain myself. I was going to have to try to make this 'chat' last as long as possible.

"Jason isn't here," I said. "I don't know where he is." I had to play along and at least pretend I had no idea why she was in my room.

"It's not Jason I'm looking for," Cherry said, in soothing tones. "I've come to talk to you, Robin. Is that okay?"

I nodded awkwardly and sat on the edge of my bed. Cherry pulled the chair from my desk over to the bed and sat very close to me. It was frustrating that her skirt was too long for me to see up. However, I had other things on my mind.

I'd never been quite this close to Cherry on my own before and it felt both intimate and unimaginably exciting. Suddenly I'd lost all power of speech. I stared dumbly into her clear blue eyes, silently willing her to kiss me. I could smell her perfume – it was sweet and subtle, like her. Some women's perfume was harsh and cloying and irritated your nostrils but this was fruity and fresh and nice. She smelled good.

The silence between us seemed to last forever. Suddenly Cherry took my hand in hers. I was sure I was trembling and, out of sheer embarrassment, I felt an overwhelming urge to snatch my hand away. It took a mighty force of will to leave my hand hanging limply in her grip.

"I'll be honest with you, Robin. Your Mum asked me to talk to you. She's very worried about you. She thinks I can help."

"Help what?" I squeaked. I had barely managed to recover the power of speech but I still had to maintain the pretence of not knowing why she was there beside me.

"Well," Cherry began, drawing out the word 'well' to an unnatural length – betraying this was a difficult situation for her too. "Your Mum wants me to speak to you about…about death, Robin. She's worried you're…you're um…you're…"

Now I actually did pull my hand away, which startled Cherry somewhat. Quickly, I grabbed both her hands in mine – under the guise of giving her the encouragement and support she needed to finish her sentence – and it felt wonderful to be assertive with her in that way.

"Go on," I said, surprised by my own boldness.

Cherry pulled her hands from mine and smoothed her skirt (even though it wasn't ruffled).

"Your mum is worried you're becoming obsessed with death, Robin. She said that ever since Marc Bolan died you've been in a sort of state of mourning and you won't stop. She just wants her old Robin back."

She folded her hands in her lap.

"Robin? Robin? Say something!" Cherry prompted.

"Huh?" I was daydreaming about trying to kiss her and imagining her reciprocating.

"Robin, your mother thinks I should talk to you because…"

Oh God! She was actually going to say it. She was going to say it was because I had a crush on her. They all knew it. It must have been so obvious. I could feel myself going red. Suddenly I wanted to be anywhere but there.

"…because, as you might know, my mother died when I was your age or perhaps even a bit younger. You're now…how old is it?"

Thank God! It *wasn't* just because I was keen on her that they'd sent her to me! I had to keep the sense of relief out of my voice when I replied.

"Fourteen. I was fourteen last July."

"Well, I was thirteen when my mum died. That's six years ago now. It was terrible when it happened, Robin, terrible. There's not a day goes by when I don't think of her but life goes on. It has to."

She took my hand again. This time it felt more comfortable, more natural. I gripped her hand and gave it a squeeze and held on manfully. It felt so good I never wanted to let go. Cherry had tears in her eyes and I could feel myself welling up in sympathy.

"Yes," I stammered. "Yes, it does."

"Are you…are you worried about your mum, Robin?" Cherry asked suddenly.

The question caught me off guard. This really wasn't about Mum – at least I didn't think it was. It was about Marc Bolan – at least, it was when it started. Then it just spiralled. The truth was I'd kept dressing in black because it became a habit. Plus, it got a reaction and one of the main effects it had was that Jason had left me alone (at least more than usual) when I was wearing black and moping about and locking myself away.

When he'd seen me depressed and down all the time, he'd also found there was no real joy to be had in teasing me or tormenting me because it made no real difference to my demeanour. It happened or it didn't happen and my outlook never changed so he gradually stopped bothering even to try to hassle me as he got absolutely nothing out of it. I kind of liked that power and I especially liked being left alone by him. But I knew I couldn't keep it up forever and I certainly hadn't anticipated the effect it would have on Mum. I didn't want to add to the stress in her life and clearly I had been making her desperate; desperate enough to send Cherry to me for this pep talk anyway.

"This isn't about Mum," I said.

"Okay," Cherry said patiently. "Do you want to tell me what this *is* about then? The dressing in black, the…"

"Why would it be about Mum? Why would you bring Mum into this?"

I probably sounded whiney but I hoped I didn't sound aggressive. I didn't mean to be aggressive – I'd never ever be aggressive with Cherry – but she'd put me on the defensive.

"Well, um…you know, the smoking, the cough, the er…" Cherry's voice trailed off.

Everyone – except Jason – always kept on about Mum's smoking and Mum's cough. They all kept saying she'd get cancer or she had cancer already. When I was younger I used to plead with her to quit but she'd wave my appeals away – usually with the same hand that was holding a burning cigarette. 'It's my only pleasure in life, Robin' she'd say. Then she'd add: 'I'll do you a deal – when the doctor tells me I have to stop, I'll stop immediately. Just like that, alright?' It was one of many 'deals' Mum offered me about quitting smoking that I knew she'd never keep.

"It's not about Mum," I repeated.

"Okay, well. I won't ask you about it anymore. But, Robin…"

Cherry stood up and sat on the bed right next to me. I felt her thigh rubbing against mine. It felt incredibly warm; warmer than I'd have ever imagined. She put her arm around me and rested her head against my head and sort of cuddled me awkwardly.

I didn't know what to do. Part of me wanted to hug her in return, to push her back onto the bed and try to kiss her using my tongue. Another part of me wanted this to stop and to stop right now. Still another part of me wanted this to stop in case Jason walked in and caught us together – a prospect that was far worse than death itself.

"Robin, listen. Just for me – and for your Mum – will you try to stop all this 'death business' and at least try to go back to how you were? To once again be the Robin we both love?"

She loves me?! Cherry loves me?! I wanted to dance around the room in ecstasy at those words but I knew I couldn't make my transformation quite that sudden. I looked down at my feet and nodded.

"I'll try," I said.

"Good lad," Cherry replied, standing up and ruffling my hair with genuine affection.

She walked to the door while I remained seated on the bed. Before leaving, she turned and smiled the nicest smile I'd ever seen on anyone anywhere. (How on earth did Jason get a girl like this?).

"And Robin…put some colourful clothes on, eh? Put all that black stuff back in the drawer, come downstairs and show your Mum the real Robin is back. See you down there, yeah?"

I nodded meekly, happier than I'd ever been while fervently hoping Cherry and I could have another one of these 'chats' soon. Cherry *loved* me – she'd said it herself and she'd said it out loud…so it had to be *true*.

Chapter 15

It was the end of November. Mum was on a high because another Royal baby had been born when Princess Anne gave birth to a son called Peter.

Arguably, though, Mum was on an even bigger high because, as a direct result of Cherry's intervention, I had finally given up dressing in black and "moping about" (as Jason put it). In fact, I'd been careful only to wear bright colours for some time to fully reinforce that I'd definitely moved on.

The sole exception was my ANL t-shirt, which I still wore with pride. Luckily, Jason's prediction had been wrong and I hadn't been beaten up for displaying it in public – although a couple of skinheads who'd spotted me wearing it did spit at me from the top deck of a passing bus.

"Christmas is coming and the goose is getting fat," my mother sang as she pottered round the house doing the cleaning. "Soon be Christmas, Robin," she called from the front room. "What would you like me to get you?"

I walked in and sat down in the big armchair. "I've not really thought about it, thanks."

Mum ambled across to me, pinched both my cheeks between thumb and forefinger and jiggled them up and down – although she didn't do it in the rough way Jason would have done. It was really more annoying than painful so I happily tolerated it as I hadn't seen Mum quite this happy for weeks. "Think carefully about what you want then, mister," Mum trilled before releasing my cheeks and ruffling my hair. "Hmm, best give you a haircut too. This unruly mop of yours is getting rather straggly. Come to the salon after school on Monday, yes? Monday afternoons are always pretty quiet. We'll cut it for you then."

"Can I have it Punk style? Spiked up?" I asked eagerly.

I'd actually thought of going somewhere else and getting it done independently but I didn't have the money. Besides, I'd never get over the earache if I didn't run it past Mum first. Now there was a chance of having it done for free.

"I don't know, Robin," Mum mused. "What would they say at school? It doesn't really give the right impression, does it?"

Well, it wasn't an outright 'no'. My heart leapt – it seemed there was a small chance Mum might actually agree. I couldn't believe my luck. She was in the best mood ever!

"It's OK, it's allowed at school," I said – not really knowing if that was true. "Simon Dixon has his hair spiked and no-one's picked him up on it. As long as it's not died blue or green, I'm pretty sure it's fine."

"Well, if you really want it like that, Robin, I guess we'll see what we can do. So, you'll come by straight from school on Monday, yes? Now, what would you like me to get you for Christmas? I don't have much money to spare but I've put a small amount aside for each of you boys."

I felt overwhelmed. Mum was always good to me but I had the feeling she wanted to make sure I was extra happy after my so-called 'death obsession phase'. I stood up and hugged her. "Thanks Mum," I said, burying my nose in her hair, the way I used to do as an infant.

"I'll have a think. Something to do with my fish tank would be brilliant, thanks. I'd really like a whole new tank, ideally. I've wanted a bigger fish tank for ages. I need something big enough to add bigger fish. In fact, that would be brill, thanks. If it's possible, that is."

I wasn't sure Mum if could afford a new tank and I really rather doubted it. At the end of the day, she actually had to get Jason something as well – it couldn't all be about me. I grabbed her by the arm and said hurriedly: "Of course, if a new tank costs too much, then just some new equipment will be fine, thanks. The heater and filter in my current tank are both getting old. They don't cost too much and a new one of either of those would be totally fab, thanks."

"I can stretch to a new fish tank, Robin, it's not a problem. Listen, it's a done deal. A new fish tank it is then."

I stepped back and looked directly into her eyes.

"Thanks Mum, that's beyond super, thanks. I really didn't know what to say."

"Pick out the one you want, write the details down on a bit of paper and leave the rest to me – and Father Christmas, of course." She laughed indulgently.

"Thanks, that's great. Really, really great."

"Well, then. I think that deserves a nice cuppa, don't you? So, how about you making me one, you little monkey?"

"Coming up," I replied, heading to the kitchen in double-quick time.

After I'd fixed Mum's tea I ran up the road as quickly as I could to Mr Ramjit's to buy up all the tropical fish magazines he had in stock. I came home with a copy of *Practical Fishkeeper Monthly* and *Tropical Fish World Magazine*.

Then I dashed up to my room to comb through each and every advertisement and review for fish tanks. Before settling on my bed I held both magazines up against the side of the tank and told the fish: "Get ready to move home soon, guys." It was probably just my imagination but I was sure 'Mr. Lucas' understood me because he came right up to the glass and hovered there for ages, blowing bubbles in my direction.

Both tropical fish mags said the same thing – get the biggest tank you could afford. If I got one that was about 18 gallons then I could expand beyond my humble Neon Tetras (and 'Mr Lucas') into Chichlids and Gouramis. Even a 14 gallon tank would be better than my current one – it all depended on what Mum could afford. I'd need a new base for a bigger tank too. It wouldn't fit on the old side table we'd bought from the second hand shop when I'd got my first tank. So that would be an added cost. I decided I'd better be extra nice when I went to see Mum on Monday for my new spiky haircut.

Chapter 16

Monday took ages to arrive – and it seemed to take even longer for school to end on the day itself – but finally it was time.

I threw my school books and homework into my beaten up *Adidas* bag and barrelled out of the front gate. Then I ran non-stop all the way to Mum's salon to get my hair spiked. I arrived totally breathless, bursting through the door, crouching and coughing to regain my composure. Mum looked round and laughed.

"Good grief, Robin. You're keen to get your hair cut, aren't you?"

I dropped my bag on the floor behind the reception desk. There was a girl at the counter with coal black hair cut in a sort of Ziggy Stardust mullet. She had thick black eye make-up trailing round the side of her head so it looked, from a distance, like she was wearing a pirate mask. She looked a lot like Siouxsie Sioux. She looked sort of scary and yet sexy at the same time. She can't have been much more than my age, I figured – she was probably 17 or 18; 19 at the most. She was smoking a menthol cigarette and looking at me as if I'd just been beamed down from another planet. I was looking back at her in much the same way.

"This is Nina," Mum said. "She's going to do your hair for you. She knows what you young folk like, these days."

I stared at Nina as she continued to smoke blithely, puffing a thin trail of minty-smoky vapour in my direction. An expression of total boredom masked whatever she might have been thinking.

"Nina, this is my son, Robin – the one I told you about. Robin, this is Nina," Mum burbled happily.

Nina waved her cigarette vaguely in my direction. It was practically a royal wave. Other than that, there was not a flicker of emotion from her.

"I thought *you* were going to do it," I said to Mum with a slight air of desperation. Mum laughed again – an indulgent chuckle.

"Me? No, no, no. Nina's the best. If you want it spiked, she's your girl!"

Nina smiled at me then – a disarming but slightly soulless grin.

"Don't worry, Robin." Nina said. "I won't bite!"

Mum cackled and used the foot pump to raise one of the barber's chairs. It felt a bit embarrassing that I still had to have the thing raised – Jason wouldn't have needed it. Mum patted the chair's comfy leather seat.

"Come on then, sit yourself down." It sounded like she was talking to a dog.

I walked over and took my place in the chair. It was amazingly comfy. I'd always thought these barber shop chairs were like astronaut's seats in a rocket ship. Whenever I was in one I had fantasies about blasting off to the moon, Venus or Mars.

Nina walked across, fag dangling from her lips – just like Mum or Jason, I thought. She put a towel round my neck and fastened it – a little too tightly. I stuck a finger into the 'collar' and loosened it. Nina added a second towel around the first one and fastened the new one equally tightly. Then she spun me round – the chair swivelled fully 180 degrees like a funfair ride – and I soon realised what was about to happen. She was going to wash my hair in the basin that had, only seconds ago, been facing me. Nina went to stub out her menthol cigarette but Mum stopped her.

"No, no," Mum cautioned. "I'll finish that for you, lovey – after all, waste not, want not."

Nina silently handed Mum her half-smoked cigarette and began running the taps behind my head. Then, wordlessly, she pushed my head back into the U-shape cut-out at the edge of the basin. My neck crashed into the porcelain and, as I fidgeted for position, Nina adjusted the taps once more. Then she tilted my head back further and I felt the water hit my forehead and scalp.

"Too hot?" Nina asked in a monotone as she sprayed me with a miniature hose she'd fixed to the taps.

"No, no, it's fine," I lied, not wanting to appear wimpish in front of a girl.

I felt Nina's fingers massaging my scalp – a brief pause while she added shampoo – then the massage resumed. I could get used to this, I thought. It felt wonderful. It certainly wouldn't have happened where I'd got my hair cut the last few times – at the place Jason now used. He went to a 'gentleman's barber' called Owen Wilson. I'd been there a few times – prodded along by Jason's comment that it was about time I started going to a "proper men's barbers – not some place run by Mum and aimed at birds and biddies."

Owen Wilson was a short, fat man who ran a one-man business in a tiny narrow shop that was more like a two-room cupboard. He looked a bit like Oliver Hardy – if Oliver Hardy had sported one of those long, thin Salvador Dali moustaches.

He always seemed like a really old bloke to me but he was probably still in his late fifties rather than his sixties. When you walked in to his barber shop you were immediately confronted by a reception desk that was more like one of those curved home bars some people put in their front rooms.

There were a couple of wooden chairs and a low coffee table piled high with magazines. Most of the mags were mid-range porn mags like *Mayfair*, *Penthouse* and *Playboy* – although there were a couple of car mags too. Jason thought it was brilliant – "Nothing like a quick butchers at some hairy fanny before you get your own hair snipped," he cackled.

I'd picked the mags up and had a furtive flick through while I waited to be called to the barber's chair. No-one stopped me or bothered me or said anything at all about me reading porn – even though I was only just thirteen on my first visit. That was a major contrast to trying to sneak a quick peek at any of the material on the top shelf in Mr Ramjit's shop.

When Owen Wilson called you up to get your hair cut, the first thing he did was take a fag out of a pack of *Embassy*, light it up and then announce: "Next gentleman, please." Nine times out of ten the entire haircut was over by the time the cigarette had burned down. Then he'd light another one, call out "Next gentleman, please," and the entire process would be repeated. Only Jason took longer than one cigarette because he always had a quiff with all the *Brylcreem*. I definitely only took one *Embassy*.

Part of the reason I'd gone to Mum's for the spike was because Owen Wilson wouldn't actually do it. He wouldn't have Punks in his shop. He'd happily do Rockers and Greasers with their quiffs and he'd do regular old blokes – but not Punks. 'Kids' (like me) could only get a military crew cut or a short back and sides. I'd had a short back and sides with a feathered fringe a few times but (despite the lure of *Mayfair* and *Penthouse*) I now really, really wanted a spike.

"All done," said Nina, pushing me upright and snapping me out of my reverie. She spun me round again and, before I had time to take in my reflection in the mirror, began to vigorously dry my hair with one of the towels she'd wrapped around my neck. Eventually, satisfied, she threw the towel on a nearby chair, put a comb in her mouth and picked up a selection of scissors. Now, granted free access to the mirror, I could see Mum in the background turning the 'Open' sign on the door to 'Closed' before disappearing out the back.

I looked at myself. My blonde hair was a straggly damp mess.

"Right then," said Nina. "Spiked, yes?"

"Yes, please," I said. "Sort of like Billy Idol, if you can," I added, trying to give her some image to work with.

Nina smiled and flicked at my hair a few times.

"It's quite fine but there's plenty of it. I think we can get it to stand up for you."

Jason would have laughed at the innuendo. I was just concerned she'd called my hair 'fine'. Was I going bald or something?

While I worried, Nina worked. She practically danced all around me, snipping here, combing there. One minute she was leaning over me – so close I could feel her breath – the next, standing back and looking at me as though I were a museum piece. It was okay when she was working behind me but a few times, when she stood in front of me to cut my fringe, her breasts were right in my face. And I do mean right there – eye height and jiggling away, like she was waving them at me.

She was wearing a white T-shirt that was quite tight and low cut and I didn't know where to look but I also couldn't stop looking. I tried to think of something else and not start turning into a giant beetroot. I don't know if Nina sensed my discomfort or had just become bored with the silence but she rescued the situation by suddenly talking about music.

"So, what music do you like, then?" she asked.

"Marc Bolan. T Rex. David Bowie." I said in a hopeful tone, eager she'd agree.

"Old guys, eh?" she laughed. "Yeah, they're pretty good, I s'pose."

She carried on snipping away.

"Who do you like?" I asked. "Siouxsie and the Banshees?" Nina laughed and stopped cutting.

"You noticed, eh?"

"Well, er…"

"Yes, I do model myself on Siouxsie Sioux. I really like her style but, musically, I prefer others."

"Such as?" Now I was enjoying this conversation.

"Oh, I dunno. Buzzcocks. Vibrators. Pistols. Damned."

"The Damned are good. I like The Pistols too," I enthused. "My brother hates them."

"I've heard about your brother," she said – a statement that surprised me so much I nearly fell off the chair.

"Really?" I supposed she must have fallen for him too – the way all women seemed to. I wondered if I should practice Jason's advice on her and tell her I couldn't stop thinking about her.

"Yeah, he sounds a right idiot!"

At that precise moment I could have happily got out of the chair and kissed her. A huge smile remained on my face for the rest of the time it took to cut my hair. Here, at last, was a girl who liked my taste in music and who (even better) thought Jason was an idiot. If only Cherry thought the same way.

Nina stood back, put the scissors and comb down and called my mother from the back room with a loud shout of "Mrs Bellamy." I looked in the mirror at the two women standing behind me.

"Hey presto," said Nina, spreading her arms wide for my mother to admire her handiwork.

My mother smiled uncertainly and nudged the back of my seat, prompting me to speak.

"I told you Nina was the best, Robin. Best little stylist I've ever employed – a real talent." Mum hugged Nina and the girl smiled and hugged her back.

"Aw, Rose, you're embarrassing me," she said - although you could tell she liked it really.

"Well now, Robin," Mum prompted. "Say something."

I tried. At first it wouldn't come. I was silent for only one reason – it was brilliant. It was beyond brilliant. Looking back at me from the mirror was myself – but it was a self that now looked exactly like a mini Billy Idol with blonde spiky hair swept up in a jaunty, rebellious, 'up yours' fashion. It was, quite simply, the best thing that had ever happened to me in my entire existence.

"Th-thank you, Nina. That's just…just…brilliant!" I stammered. "Really, really…*brilliant!*"

Nina put a hand on my shoulder and squeezed affectionately.

"Aw, thanks, sweetheart. You enjoy it – it looks great on you."

Yes, it did, I thought. It really honestly did. And the best thing of all was that Jason was absolutely 100% guaranteed to totally and utterly and monumentally hate it!

Chapter 17

"What the fuck happened to you?" asked Jason when he first set eyes on my new spiky haircut. "Get your fingers stuck in the plug socket?" he cackled.

"Piss off," I said, quickly running up the stairs towards the sanctuary of my bedroom. The new haircut gave me a confidence I didn't know I had.

"What did you just say, you little shitbag?" he yelled, preparing to chase after me. "Who the fuck d'you think you're talking to like that? Come here and…"

"…and what?" I heard Mum say. "Leave the boy alone. Can't you be pleased for your own brother for once? He loves his new haircut. Had it done at my place."

"Looks like a fucking bog brush," Jason sneered. "I'm going out."

Mum had undoubtedly saved me a beating but I'd also surprised myself by the sheer boldness changing my look had produced from somewhere deep inside me. The spiky hair cut felt like a new weapon in my otherwise minimal armoury. I almost felt brave enough to take Jason on face-to-face. *Almost.*

Back in my bedroom, I stared at myself in the full length mirror and I liked what I saw. A scrawny kid, certainly, but a kid made more imposing by a blonde spiky mop that seemed to issue its own challenge to all who gazed upon it.

However, I still needed to complete the look to achieve its full effect. My ANL t-shirt went well with the spike but my school trousers were totally out of place. There were adverts in the *NME* listing places where you could send off to buy bondage pants or PVC trousers. I figured I'd get a pair of each.

If I bought postal orders at the Post Office I wouldn't need to ask Mum for a cheque. Thus, it would be a done deal when my gear arrived in the post. I thought I'd get some *DayGlo* socks too – some bright yellow ones. I already had my *Vans* but maybe a pair of DMs or some punked-up brothel creepers might be a good look too. Then *no-one* would mess with me. Even Jason might think twice. And the school bullies. Maybe if I got steel toe-capped DMs, I could even fight back. Just go mental on them. Do or die! I might even win. The very prospect was intoxicating.

Suddenly there was a knock on the door. S*hit*! It had better not be Jason returning. What could I say? Sorry, I didn't mean to say 'Piss off'? No, that wouldn't work. I never said 'Piss off' – you must have mis-heard me? I actually only said 'Please, leave off.' Yes, that might work.

"Robin?" Thank God, it was just Mum.

"Hang on," I yelled. "Not decent."

I glanced round the room in a panic, trying urgently to make sure nothing was out of place – no porn mags peeping out of board game boxes, my best clothes not lying in heaps on the floor. It all seemed okay.

"Come in." I yelled, seating myself on the bed, trying to look a picture of innocence.

Mum opened the door and walked in. She smiled at me. For once, she wasn't smoking. She walked over to my fish tank and stood by it, arms folded.

"So, how much bigger does it need to be?" she asked, looking at the tank.

I stood up, walked over and put an arm around her. 'Mr Lucas' came to the side of the tank and blew bubbles at us.

"Are you sure, Mum?" I asked. She put an arm around me in return.

"Of course I'm sure, Robin. There's nothing I'd rather do than buy you a new fish tank for Christmas. You deserve it."

Where had this come from? First the haircut – the best gift I'd ever had. Now the fish tank. Why was she being so nice to me all at once? And *why* did I deserve it? I hadn't done especially well at school. There was no real reason…*unless*. A wave of nausea washed over me. Her smoking. Her cough. Could it be?

"Mum, you're…you're…" I stammered.

"I'm what, Robin?" She squeezed me tightly.

"You're…you are *alright* aren't you?"

What would I do if she…if she…left us? I'd be on my own. No, worse, I'd be alone with Jason. The thought was unbearable.

"I'm what, love?" Mum prompted.

"You are okay, aren't you? You know, the doctor…your smoking…I mean…"

Mum laughed and hugged me tightly.

"Oh, Robin, Robin. You silly boy! No, I'm not dying! Yes, the doctor said I should cut down on my smoking but I'm perfectly okay. Don't you worry your head about anything like that."

I hugged her tightly. All was well with the world.

"So, how much bigger do you want this fish tank?" she asked, eyes wide with interest.

I broke away and measured the space for her with my hands.

"About this big, thanks. That's 14 gallons. I know it sounds a lot but it's not much bigger than this, really. 18 gallons would be ideal but tanks that size are a bit expensive. Either way, it will need a new base. This table isn't strong enough. Plus, it's too low. It would be nice to have the fish at head height and not have to crouch down all the time. I mean, if you can afford 18 gallons, that is. 14 gallons is equally brilliant."

"Well, just write down what you need, dear. Let's go for 18 and a new base, shall we? Father Christmas owes me a few favours."

I bristled at her final sentence but tried not to show it. I knew in some ways she wanted me to remain her 'little boy' forever and the 'Father Christmas' stuff was only a part of that. Still, an 18 gallon tank and a brand new base to boot! All my Christmases were about to come at once – and at Christmas too!

"Thanks Mum, you're the best."

"So they tell me."

She walked to the door and paused, turning back to face me.

"Talking of fish, Jason is bringing Cherry back for tea tonight. How about I give you some money and you can run to the chippy and get us all a fish supper?"

My face lit up even more – if that were even possible. Fish and chips – my all-time favourite grub – *and* Cherry (who would be seeing my new hair style for the very first time).

"Thanks Mum. Deal!"

Pedro's was the best chippy in our area and it was within easy walking distance. Every time I went there I remembered what Jason said about buying a house – "always make sure you've got a decent pub and a decent chippy in walking distance and all the bases are covered." – not that either of us could ever afford to buy a house.

I loved *Pedro's*. I always reckoned, if I had to, I could live on fish and chips for my entire life. I'd eat it happily every single day and never ever get tired of it. I loved fish – both to look at and to eat (although I only ever actually ate it fried from the chippy or as fish fingers).

It was funny when Mum sent me to *Pedro's* to get a fish supper for the four of us because we each had a different order. Mum had plaice, I had haddock, Jason had cod and Cherry had something called Rock Salmon. Without fail, Jason would make fun of Cherry's choice every time it was mentioned.

"Rock Salmon? It's not real salmon, you know. It's catfish. Got a great big bone down the middle. It's pet food. What d'you order that for?"

"Leave the girl alone." Mum would say. "Cherry can have whatever she wants. She's a guest in this house."

"The only bone you need, love, is right here in my trousers," Jason would tell Cherry, gyrating around like he was Elvis. Despite herself, Cherry would laugh and Mum would get angry.

"Jason, you are so vulgar the entire time. I didn't bring you up that way. I don't know where you get it from, I really don't."

Jason would ignore her and continue his rant about Rock Salmon.

"At least it's got the word 'Rock' in it, I suppose. Rock and roll fish, eh? Bill Scaley. Guppy Holly. Little Pilchard." Then he would start singing: "Rock around the dock tonight…"

It was actually quite funny sometimes and we would often all end up laughing, even Mum. When he was clowning around like that it was actually possible to briefly forget he was horrible most of the time – to me, anyway. However, it wasn't going to happen tonight as Rock Salmon wasn't on the menu. When that happened, Cherry had two cod roe instead. That caused a further inevitability – Cherry would only ever eat one roe and Jason would scoff the spare one (in practically one gulp). One time when that happened, Cherry offered the spare one to me first and there was an almighty row.

"Wasted on that tit," Jason sneered before I'd answered that I didn't want it. Even though I was curious, I didn't dare say 'yes' in front of Jason and end up depriving him of it.

"You've never tried it, Robin," Mum prompted. "Go on, give it a taste, love. It's quite nice."

Cherry cut a piece from the roe and slid it carefully onto my plate. It actually looked pretty appetising in its thick golden batter. I felt three pairs of eyes on me as I cut the piece Cherry had given me in half and lifted the fork to my mouth.

"Go on, then. Eat it, you knob-end." Jason barked.

I chewed the roe a few times and swallowed. It was really, really nice but I couldn't say so in case Cherry gave me the rest and Jason lost out. They all looked at me expectantly like I was Egon Ronay about to award some dining stars.

"It's…it's not bad," I said nonchalantly.

"Would you like the rest?" Cherry asked.

"You what?" Jason snapped. "You're giving *my* roe to that cretin?"

"I think you'll find it's my roe," Cherry replied, angered by Jason's possessiveness. "I can give it to whoever I want."

"Yeah, I've heard those rumours!" Jason sneered.

Cherry raised her hand as if to smack him then realised where she was and, seeing my mother staring open-mouthed at the pair of them, immediately calmed down.

"Sorry Mrs B," Cherry said apologetically, scowling at Jason.

"I'll have it," Mum said. "I like a nice bit of roe once in a while." And then she forced herself to eat it – even though she probably didn't want it – just so Jason didn't get it.

So, now I had roe again for Cherry – as well as the plaice, haddock and cod for the rest of us. I ran home clutching the big paper bag of piping hot booty close to my chest. I could picture the scene just before I got in – Mum would have the oven on in case things needed re-heating and she'd be putting out the salt, ketchup and *Sarson's*. Cherry would be laying the cutlery on the table. Jason would be smoking a cigarette and watching them work.

I raced up our front path and was surprised to see no sign of the *Guzzi*. I went down the side path to the kitchen door and burst in. Mum was on her own in the kitchen, setting the table. She looked up at me.

"Sorry, Robin. Jason's just phoned. They've changed their plans. Apparently, they're eating at Cherry's house tonight."

"But I've just bought all this," I protested, holding up the bag of food.

"I know, he's a selfish so-and-so, isn't he? If only he'd told me earlier, I'd have saved half the money. What have you got anyway?"

"The usual but it's cod roe, not Rock Salmon, for Cherry."

"Well then," Mum smiled. "How about we have a cod roe each with our fish and chips and I'll give *his* piece to the birds."

I smiled. This was perfect. Just Mum and I – no Jason – and a piece of cod roe for each of us along with our fish. Bliss! Cherry could see my new hair cut some other time.

Chapter 18

It was December before Cherry saw my new haircut. I thought she'd be round sooner but she and Jason seemed to be spending more and more time away from our house lately.

It was now only three weeks until Christmas and school was about to end. This was a time of year I loved. All the shops had coloured lights and tinsel and trees and decorations and everywhere felt on the verge of a party the entire time. *Slade* and *Wizzard* were played over and over on the radio. Some of our neighbours had a display of multi-coloured fairy lights all around their front door and surrounding their window frames. One of them even had a plastic snowman all lit up in the front garden.

There was loads of hype for some American film called *Star Wars*. Moy said his Dad had seen it months earlier on a visit to the States and added that we absolutely must see it too. I wasn't as keen but I said I'd probably go along to keep Moy company.

One thing I did enjoy were all the toy adverts all over Saturday morning TV. Board games and *Action Man* and *Scalextric* proliferated. I used to watch the Saturday morning kids' TV show, *Tiswas*, mainly for the ads in-between. Even though I knew I was getting a new fish tank, it was still addictive to see all the new products on offer and imagine I somehow might get given some of those too. Jason walked past the TV once when *Tiswas* was on.

"You gawking at that Sally James bird again, are you, you little tosser?" he laughed.

I craned my neck to see past him.

"She looks well dirty," he laughed. Then, turning towards the screen, he undid his zip and shoved his groin at Sally's face. "There you go, sugar – a nice bit of breakfast saveloy for you. Chew on that, sweet cheeks."

He thrust himself rhythmically at the screen until the picture changed to one of the co-presenter, Chris Tarrant. Jason spun round, zipped up his trousers and wagged a finger at the screen. "Oi, that's not for you, Tarrant – even if you do look a fat poof!" Then Jason cuffed me round the ear – playfully by his standards – before vanishing in a roar of the *Guzzi*.

Now it was Sunday night and Cherry was coming round for a Sunday roast. Mum's Sunday roasts were the best. Usually it was chicken but sometimes it was pork with all the crispy crackling. Tonight, however, she was doing a rib of beef with Yorkshire pudding because Cherry once said Mum's Yorkshires were the best on Earth.

Mum never used *Bisto* and always made her own gravy. Her potatoes were always golden and crispy and somehow she even made the greens taste nice. We were also having *Arctic Roll* for afters. It was a proper slap-up feast. Not even Jason missed one of Mum's roasts if he could help it. We were also having wine – Jason was supposed to bring that.

"Get something decent, will you, Jason," Mum had warned him. "Not that *Mateus* rubbish."

"But Cherry likes *Mateus*," Jason protested.

"Cherry's getting roast beef and Yorkshires – she can be happy with that. I'm not having my food ruined by cheap. nasty wine. Get something French and red – I'll give you the money back. Robin, fetch my purse."

"You're alright," Jason said. "I can stretch to a bottle of plonk." Mum nodded.

And now they were here. I heard the *Guzzi* burbling as Jason pulled up. I ran to my upstairs vantage point to try to watch Cherry dismount. Unfortunately, on this occasion, Cherry was in a pair of velvet trousers – well, I guess it was winter now. Still, she'd teamed her trousers with some kinky-looking knee-length white boots – just like the ones the *Pan's People* dancers wore on *Top Of The Pops*. That was still something of a secret thrill. I raced back downstairs to greet them. What would Cherry make of my hair, I wondered?

I hovered behind Mum as she opened the front door. Jason, waving a bottle of wine wrapped in tissue paper as though it were an invitation, stood back and allowed Cherry to enter ahead of him. As soon as she'd crossed the threshold, I popped my head round from behind my mother.

"Hi Cherry," I called cheerily.

"Oh, my God," Cherry exclaimed, putting a hand up to her mouth. "Robin? Is that really you? Oh, my God."

I beamed at her. I wasn't sure what to make of her outburst – was it an 'oh, my God, what the hell have you done to your hair?' or was it an 'oh, my God, you look great'? I stood grinning insanely like the village idiot, waiting for any further response. Jason walked in and clipped me smartly round the top of the head.

"He looks like a fucking bog brush. You don't have to be polite, Chezza. Just tell him straight. Little twat lost a fight with a lawnmower."

Jason cackled, pushed past all of us and headed straight for the kitchen. "Smells good, Mum" he called.

"Good evening to you too," Mum muttered. Then she hugged Cherry. "Come on in, my lovely. I really don't know how you put up with that son of mine, I really don't."

Cherry smiled meekly at Mum, who turned and went into the kitchen after Jason. "Have you got a spare ciggie, Jason, love?" I heard her asking.

Cherry ruffled my hair affectionately and bent down to whisper in my ear.

"I *love* your hair, Robin. Don't pay any attention to Jason. It looks great on you, it really does. It makes you look very grown up."

Then she kissed the top of my head. I could have fainted. Cherry actually kissed me and she did it in secret, away from Jason's line of vision. She called me 'grown up'. What could this mean? Could she actually fancy me now – even just a tiny bit? Could my new haircut have done the trick? Could I actually now have a sniff of a chance with Cherry? I stood looking at her, speechless. My limbs seemed not to want to respond to my thoughts. I was blocking Cherry's path to the kitchen but I was saying nothing. I was like a statue – an ice sculpture that just wouldn't melt. The moment was becoming awkward. Suddenly Cherry grabbed my forearm.

"Robin, are you…are you okay now?" she asked with real concern. It took me a while to twig what she was going on about.

"You know, if you ever want to talk…" she continued.

Of course, the 'death obsession' phase. *That's* what she meant.

"I'm fine, thanks," I spluttered. "Honestly, that's over. Finished. Thanks for your help with it, though."

She ruffled my hair again and took me by the hand.

"Glad to hear it. Shall we go and eat?"

I walked hand-in-hand with Cherry into the kitchen. Mum and Jason were bustling about, taking cutlery out of the drawer and hauling plates down from the cupboards. Each of them had a lighted gasper pursed in their lips, their eyes screwed up in a mix of concentration and subliminal avoidance of cigarette smoke. Jason looked across at Cherry and me.

"What are you holding hands with that spastic for? He can walk by himself can't he?" he growled.

Cherry and I released each other's hands as suddenly as if we'd been caught canoodling behind the bikes sheds.

"Give us a hand here, will you, LB? Come on, set the table."

I took the cutlery from his grasp – four knives, four forks, four spoons tumbling from his large hands into my small ones. Inevitably, I dropped some. They bounced on the floor with a harsh metallic clatter.

"You fucking flid!" Jason yelled.

Cherry scrambled to pick the dropped cutlery up.

"It was an accident, Jason. He didn't mean to do it." Cherry cautioned, defending me. It brought tears to my eyes that she was standing up to Jason on my behalf.

Suddenly, my mother was on Jason, smacking him repeatedly with her rubber gloves which she held bunched in her right fist. Jason put up an arm to defend himself although, in truth, they were hardly killer blows.

"Leave Robin alone, will you, you damn bully? I am so sick of this. You disgust me."

Mum had totally lost her cool. She wouldn't stop hitting him. Cherry and I stood back and watched – Cherry plainly embarrassed while I felt an odd mixture of utter horror fused with a secret pleasure that Jason was being physically attacked. Jason suddenly started laughing – as if this was the funniest thing that had ever happened.

"Get off me, you mad woman." Jason cackled, flinging his lit cigarette in the washing up bowl before using both hands to fend Mum off. "You're nuts. You've lost it."

Mum carried on hitting him. Now his contemptuous laughter turned to outright scorn.

"You're a mental case, Mum. Truly. Frankly, it's been coming for years."

Mum stopped hitting Jason and stood frozen, looking at him in a cold, unsettling silence. Eventually, she found her voice.

"Don't you dare speak to me like that in my own home or..."

"Or what?" Jason challenged. "I put as much money on the table as you do these days. Every quid you bring in, I match it – in fact, I double it most weeks."

"And that gives you the right to talk to me – and your own brother – like we're nothing, does it? Tell me, what sewer did you crawl out from? Because those are not my values, my boy. If your father was here..."

"Yeah? Well, he's not, is he? And we all know *why*..."

There was an extended silence once more. Cherry took my hand again. I gripped on tightly and squeezed. The only thing I could think was that, if this got any worse, I might never see Cherry again.

"Get out!" Mum said quietly.

"Now, listen, Mum," Jason replied, doing that calming gesture you use when someone is on a ledge and threatening to jump; holding both palms up at her like a puppeteer with an invisible marionette.

"Get out!" Mum screamed – so loudly I thought my ears might

burst. I actually put both arms round Cherry's waist and clung to her. I was excruciatingly embarrassed for her – and I didn't want to lose her, either.

"Okay, if that's what you want. Fuck it, I'm going," Jason snarled. "You want to get your head examined, Mum. Seriously."

"Out!" The command was accompanied by a raised arm and an outstretched finger, pointing directly to the door.

Jason grabbed Cherry and wrenched her roughly away from me, manhandling her as though the argument were somehow all her fault.

"Cherry is welcome to stay, if she wishes," Mum said coldly. "You're not."

Cherry allowed herself to be hauled to the doorway, briefly looking back balefully towards my mother and me.

"I'm sorry Mrs B," Cherry wailed, on the edge of tears.

"Me too, Cherry, love. Me too." My mother spoke firmly, through gritted teeth.

Then, almost as soon as they'd arrived, Cherry and Jason were gone. Mum sat down at the kitchen table and put her head in her hands. I walked up behind her and put both my hands on her shoulders. One of Mum's hands immediately snaked back towards me, feeling for my one of my hands. Finding my left hand, she gripped my fingers and squeezed weakly.

"I'm sorry, Robin," she said in a pitiful tone. "I'm so very sorry."

I took hold of her hand and, with my free hand, began to smooth her hair – as though calming a distressed puppy.

"Mum?"

"Yes?"

"Can we still have dinner, even though it's just the two of us?"

"I don't know, Robin. I honestly don't know. I don't think I know anything anymore."

Chapter 19

In the end, Mum served a plate of food only to me. She said she'd lost her appetite although much later she made herself a piece of toast.

Because it was now only me eating dinner, I was allowed to have my food on a tray in front of the TV. I also got extra meat, extra spuds, extra gravy, extra Yorkshire puddings – extra everything. I scoffed my food in front of *Jim'll Fix It*. Watching that show reminded me of another argument Mum and Jason had fought out not so long ago. We'd all been watching telly when Jimmy Savile had appeared fronting a road safety campaign. "Clunk click every trip," he'd said in that weird accent of his, waving his cigar about and gurning at the camera.

"Look at that fucking nonce," Jason had sneered. "As if anyone needs to take any notice of anything that ugly old cunt has to say."

Mum slammed her fist down on her armchair.

"Jason. Do you always have to think the worst of everyone. Have you *nothing* nice to say about *anybody*? And your language – I swear it's getting worse."

Jason shrugged.

"He looks like a frigging nonce, I'm telling you. Just look at him. Pervy-looking creep."

"The man does a lot of work for charity. You can't go by looks alone, you know."

"Greasy cigar-munching tosspot," Jason continued. "I tell you, if you'd set out to design a kiddie fiddler on a bit of graph paper from scratch then this weirdo prick is precisely what you'd end up with – a fucking freak in a tracksuit perving round the school playground. Needs a damn good kicking, if you ask you me."

"You're too quick to judge sometimes," Mum admonished. "You should give people a chance, you know."

"Not cunts." Jason sneered, standing up to leave the room. "Cunts deserve nothing."

And now, here I was, watching Jimmy Savile on the TV again and all it did was remind me of Mum and Jason fighting. Savile had some little kid perched next to him on the arm of his giant red armchair. He was asking the kid 'was that you on that there film clip doing all that amazing stuff then?' when plainly he knew it was.

The kid nodded, apparently enjoying the pantomime. Savile then reached over and presented him with his 'Fix It badge' and the kid looked as happy as a pig in shite. Then Savile picked up a piece of paper, grinned at the camera and said 'now then, now then, I've got a letter…' and that was the cue for the first kid to be unceremoniously removed and another one shoved in to take its place. It all seemed so routine and insincere. Somehow I had the idea that, in this case at least, Jason might be closer to the truth than Mum.

I finished my meal and took my plate through to the kitchen. I'd licked it clean. It didn't even look as if it needed to go in the washing up bowl. Mum was sitting at the table and smoking while doing the crossword in today's paper. She looked up and smiled.

"Blimey, Robin. You were hungry. I'm glad it didn't all go to waste. I can give the rest to the birds."

"Can I still have some *Arctic Roll*?" I asked hopefully.

"'Course you can, love," Mum smiled. "Are you sure you haven't got a tapeworm?"

I smiled back and took the *Arctic Roll* out of the deep freeze. As I was opening the pack and cutting a slice, Mum called over asking me to help her out with the crossword.

"Rubbish in four, beginning with J."

"Junk."

"Oh yes, bloody Americanisms creeping in everywhere these days. Crustacean in seven – starts with L and ends –er."

"Lobster."

"Good grief, Robin. Are you sure you didn't set this crossword? Right then, I'll try you with another. Re-marry illegally in six – I've got no letters for that one yet."

I thought for a while. I concentrated really hard while I put the *Arctic Roll* back in the freezer and fetched myself a teaspoon.

"Bigamy," I shouted in sudden triumph. "To re-marry against the law is bigamy."

Mum put her pen down and applauded.

"Really, Robin, you're a genius, I swear. How do you even know that? At your age as well."

"I read a lot," I said matter-of-factly. Partly that was true – the whole family knew me to be a bookworm (although I must admit *The Silmarillion* was proving a step beyond and, as much as I enjoyed Tolkien, I didn't plan to finish it). However, in this case, I'd actually got the answer from a Marx Brothers movie I'd seen on TV the previous Christmas. In one scene, Groucho was asked by a fat woman if he'd marry her. He'd said he was already married but that, yes, he'd still marry her. She'd said 'but that's bigamy' and he'd replied 'well, that's bigamy too!' I'd got the joke and Jason hadn't and thus I'd remembered it ever since. I *loved* the Marx Brothers.

"You've got a good future ahead of you, Robin," Mum said wistfully. "You're a good lad, you really are. Go on, take your *Arctic Roll* back to the front room – go and enjoy some more telly."

I walked back to the settee feeling ten feet tall. Savile had finished and *The Muppets* had come on instead. John Cleese was their special guest. I remembered him from *Fawlty Towers*, which was the most brilliant sitcom ever.

Despite Jason causing aggro with Mum, this was turning into quite a good evening for me. Later, I was even allowed to stay up and watch a *Hammer* horror film on TV – this, despite it being Sunday. The film was called *Twins Of Evil*. It was properly scary and the women in it were actual twins and they got their actual tits out for the camera and flashed them about properly so you got a really decent butchers. I couldn't wait to tell everyone at school I'd been allowed to stay up and see a *Hammer* – including tits. I went to bed inordinately happy.

It must have been the early hours of the morning when the landing light came on just outside my bedroom. It was Jason arriving home – about twenty-three sheets to the wind by the sound of it. Harsh electric light permeated through the gap in my partly open bedroom door, illuminating a poster of The Jam on stage. I could see Paul Weller leaping in the air with his guitar, both legs kicking up beneath him.

"Oi, Little Bastard, are you awake?" a voice slurred, entering my room and coming ever closer until I could smell the alcohol permeating out of every pore.

"Yeah, 'course you're awake, you little shithead. You *wanker*."

I decided the best option in this scenario was to pretend to be asleep – no matter how dangerous the tactic appeared it was probably far safer than actually confronting a paralytic Jason face-to-face. If I ignored him he might just get bored and go away. The only question was whether to pretend to snore not – *which* would look more convincing? If the snores were too theatrical – like a ham actor – he'd be likely to suss me immediately and whatever was coming my way would be ten times worse. However, if I didn't snore, would he get the message that I was 'asleep', drunk as he was? I decided on a hybrid option and began to emit a vague and indistinct murmur. I felt my bed sink and heard it creaking in protest as Jason sat down heavily beside me.

"Hey, LB. Oi, *fuckhead*," Jason cooed in my ear. "Little Bastard." Now he was singing. "Wakey, wakey, you little arsehole!" Then he started laughing. I could feel the bed shaking as he did it. "Oh well, go and fuck yourself then," he eventually muttered. "You're no fucking fun."

I felt his weight lift from the bed as he stood up. I dared not open my eyes. I produced a false moan and turned away – convincingly, I hoped – to face the wall.

"Hey, LB, your fishies look mighty thirsty."

I didn't really take the words in.

Briefly, silence reigned. Then I heard Jason shuffling over to the far side of my bedroom. I hardly dared breathe. The silence in the room was now so deep I thought I might explode. Then I heard Jason undo his flies. What the hell was he doing now? Then I heard the lid to my fish tank smacking against the wall as he threw it open. Then – horrifically – I heard the sound of liquid pouring rapidly into the tank. It took an extended moment for me to fully comprehend what he was doing – mainly because I didn't believe he had actually done *that*. My worst fears were confirmed when I heard him half-talking and half-singing to himself.

"Drinkie, drinkie little fishies. There you go thirsty fishes. Some yummy yellow water for you. Drink it all up thirsty little fishies."

When he'd finished he walked over to the bedroom door and called out to me.

"Sweet dreams, LB."

I dared not move and it took me a long time to be certain he'd gone. I didn't trust he wasn't waiting in the doorway, ready to ambush me when I showed the slightest sign of being awake. By the time I did pluck up the courage to get out of bed, it was too late to save my fish.

Chapter 20

The next day at school was a blank. I spent it in an angry fog of hatred; an intensity of venom I didn't know I possessed.

When I'd got up in the morning, I'd taken a quick glance at the fish tank using only my peripheral vision. I didn't dare to look at the ruined tank full on or I would have gone to the kitchen, plucked a carving knife from the drawer, gone back upstairs and plunged it straight between Jason's ribs.

From the corner of my eye I could see the lid to the tank was still open and several tiny bodies were floating stiffly on the surface of the discoloured water. One of them was 'Mr Lucas'. I dressed rapidly and went downstairs for a cursory breakfast of *Weetabix*. Then I gathered my things and went to school. As I left, I spat very deliberately on the petrol tank of the *Guzzi*.

There was no sign of Jason when I returned home. Instead, Mum was waiting for me, her face a picture of concern.

"Robin, love, I don't know how to tell you this…"

I knew what was coming. I stared at her blankly as I unpacked my homework from my *Adidas* bag. Mum continued hesitantly.

"Your…um…your fish are dead. Robin, I'm so sorry. I went into your room and the lid of the tank was open. I thought that was unusual and, when I got closer, I saw them all floating on the top, poor little mites."

I continued unpacking my school bag in silence. If Jason had been there, I just might have launched myself at him. Mum was concerned by my seemingly blank reaction.

"Did you…did you know about this Robin?" Mum asked cautiously.

Now I looked straight at her. I was so very tempted to tell her what Jason had done but years of instinctive covering for him kicked in. Despite my better judgment, I lied.

"No, well, not exactly. I knew something was wrong but I didn't have time to do anything about it or I'd have been late for school. I woke up late, lifted the lid – there was nothing I could do. I think something happened to the filter."

I looked suitably downcast but I hated myself for letting Jason off the hook.

"Well, it's just as well you're getting a new tank for Christmas then," Mum said kindly. She stepped forward and put an arm around me. "It's such a pity we couldn't get your fish out of that old tank and into the new one before it failed. Well, it looks as though we'll need to get you some new fish to go with that new tank. Oh, Robin, I'm so sorry."

Her kindness nearly tipped me over the edge and started me blubbing but my anger at Jason prevented any tears from flowing.

"Thanks Mum," I said and hugged her tightly.

"You're taking this very well, Robin, I must say. I dreaded telling you. I thought you'd be devastated."

I knew what was worrying her most – it was my recent so-called 'death obsession'. She was concerned the fish dying would trigger a relapse and she'd once again have to witness me wandering around the house dressed entirely in black and being morbid. Well, that wasn't going to happen. I now knew what was going to happen – and I planned to do it that very night. Enough was enough.

"Have a seat Robin, I'll fix you some tea. How about jam sandwiches and hot chocolate?"

"Sounds great, thanks Mum," I said, pulling out the nearest chair. "Where's Jason?" I asked as casually as I could muster.

"Hmm? Oh, still at work, I expect. Or round at Cherry's. He's practically living there these days, isn't he?"

"I wish he was," I muttered irritably.

Mum came over and placed a hand on my shoulder.

"You know, it's terrible to admit it – and please don't tell him – but sometimes I find myself thinking the exact same thing."

Later that night I put my plan into action. I'd set my alarm to go off at 2am and placed it carefully in my partially open bedside cabinet drawer. I figured it would be loud enough to wake me but not to wake anyone else. Jason was a heavy sleeper but Mum wasn't. She'd be the one I had to worry about.

I was in the blackest unconscious void when a somewhat muffled alarm gradually dragged me into wakefulness. At first I was so sleepy I couldn't figure out what was happening – and my instinct was to go straight back to sleep. Then, in one heart-stopping instant, it all came flowing back: Jason, my fish, my anger – still burning, still fuelling a desire for revenge. I opened the drawer, snatched the clock and silenced it. I sat on the edge of my bed, my head swimming. I'd never been awake at 2am before – except when I was unwell and off school. Everything felt strange and unreal at that hour. The room was cold and the bed was still warm. It was so very tempting to climb back beneath the covers and forget what I was about to do. However, my desire for revenge was overwhelming.

I put my slippers on and pulled my dressing gown over my pyjamas. There was an old torch in the bottom drawer of my bedside cabinet. The beam was weak but the batteries were relatively new. It would have to do, I supposed. I walked to the window, pulled back the curtains and peeped out.

The street was quiet, nothing stirred. It looked oddly hypnotic. Now for the difficult part, I thought – getting in and out of the house without being detected. I gritted my teeth. This would call for the ultimate in stealth and concentration.

I opened my bedroom door carefully. It had a tendency to creak if you did it too slowly so I held my breath and swung it open reasonably quickly. Silence – of the most golden variety. I poked my head into the corridor. I could actually hear Jason snoring. Good. Mum was the real hazard, though. I stepped gingerly out of my room.

Some of the floorboards would groan if I stood on them. The same was true of several of the stairs. I'd either have to skip out the creaky stairs completely or make sure I only stood on the very edges so they wouldn't squeak. It was like negotiating a minefield – all the while accompanied by the surprisingly loud sound of Jason's snores. Even his snoring sounded arrogant.

Somehow I made it to the bottom of the stairs without waking either of the sleepers. Now for the front door. I darted into the kitchen and snatched the spare key. Then I hurried to the front door. The key felt cold in my fingers and I fumbled to get it into the lock. The door stuck a bit as I pulled it towards me. When it did finally open (with a judder) the force made the letterbox rattle. I gasped and held my breath. I didn't dare turn round and look behind me so I just stood there listening intently. They must still be asleep, I told myself. Okay, I'd come this far – now I just needed to get this done and go back to bed. A blast of cold air hit me in the face.

I stepped into the night. This must have been how the astronauts felt stepping onto the moon, I thought. Alien territory. I closed the front door slowly, wedging it in its frame rather than shutting it completely – I couldn't risk the door juddering again when I opened it on my return. I walked past the *Guzzi*, my eyes narrowing at the very sight of it. I'll be seeing you in a minute, I thought.

Now for the difficult bit – getting inside the garage. This was the riskiest part of all. Somehow, I had to open the garage door (which was almost certain to clang) and get in and out of the garage without Jason, my Mum or any of our neighbours seeing me. Opening the garage – and being in there – was the time I was most likely to be caught. If that happened, I'd already decided to pretend I was sleep-walking.

It seemed unlikely and I wasn't even sure if sleep-walking was real outside of cheap novels and Hollywood B-movies but it was the only defence I'd have. I'd got the idea because there'd been some bloke in the papers who'd murdered his wife in his sleep. His defence was he'd been sleep-walking and the judge had actually believed him. There was an outcry and nobody anywhere thought he was telling the truth except the judge and some doctor who specialised in what the newspaper article called 'sleep disorders'.

I turned the handle to the garage – we never kept it locked. The metal handle was ice cold. Although metal, the door was very light thanks to its springs. They were the things that made it clang so much though. I only raised the door sufficiently for me to roll under it – I dared not lift it all the way. Thankfully, there was only a minimal noise. I rolled underneath, not caring how grubby my dressing gown became. I hurt my hip as I rolled over the torch I'd concealed in my pocket.

Once inside the garage, I retrieved the torch. It was so cold in there I could actually see my breath. I shone the weak beam around. I knew exactly what I was looking for but it took a moment to get my bearings. The ping-pong table we never used was leaning against the wall to my right.

There were several boxes of things we'd accumulated over the years and never bothered to take to the tip. They were stacked hither and thither, like an obstacle course. To my left were some shelves Dad had built and on the lowest shelf was exactly what I wanted: Dad's old tool kit. It was a blue metal contraption with a handle on top and two drawers that folded outwards automatically as you opened it.

I put the torch down and opened the tool kit. Picking up the torch, I soon found what I was looking for – a large metal file with sharp teeth and a vicious looking point at one end. I shoved the file in my pocket. It felt heavy and dangerous. I worried it might fall out and make a loud clanging sound on the stone floor. I stuffed it further into my pocket and the point began to rip through the material of my dressing gown. I closed the tool box, gathered up the torch and rolled back outside. The garage door now made a huge clang as I shut it – a dreadful sound that seemed to echo right up the entire street. It must have seemed louder to me, though, as no-one stirred. Good. Now for the final act.

I walked over to the *Guzzi*, crouched down, took out the file and shone the torch on the front wheel. I spotted a cable that I thought must be the front brake. I concluded it was the brake cable as it was in the exact same place as it would be on my bicycle. Then I turned the torch off and began to saw away at the cable with the file. I don't know how long I sawed for or how much damage I did. I was just motivated by hatred and anger and the overwhelming need for revenge – it was like I was possessed by it. The cable made a squealing metallic sound as I sawed. I felt along the area I'd attacked with my fingers and it felt frayed. I didn't saw all the way through the cable though – I wasn't sure I could – but I'd definitely done some damage and I decided it was enough. Enough was enough. Take that, Jason. Now we were *even*.

I ran for the front door. I pushed it open while holding the letterbox steady to stop it flapping. Once inside, I closed the door, flipped the latch and returned the spare front door key to the kitchen. Now to get back up to my bedroom without being seen. I had the torch in one pocket and the file in the other. I'd now have to walk upstairs in complete darkness or my sleep-walking defence would crumble.

I made it to the landing and suddenly realised I couldn't hear any snoring from Jason's room. I could feel my heart beating in both my chest and my throat at the very same time. I stood frozen on the spot for what seemed like an aeon. Then, resigned, I made a sudden dash for my room and closed the door behind me as quietly as I could. Then I waited. Silence. I exhaled. I went to the bedside cabinet and opened the middle drawer. I wrapped the file in an old t-shirt and placed it carefully at the bottom of the drawer. The torch went in the top drawer. I took off my dressing gown and stuffed it under the bed. I kicked off my slippers and sat down heavily on the bed. The whole episode felt exactly like a dream – or, more accurately, a nightmare. If I hadn't been so cold I might have actually thought it really was just a dream after all. I glanced at my empty fish tank and concluded I'd done the right thing.

I climbed beneath the bedclothes and shivered. Tiredness overwhelmed me. I fell asleep instantly, proud of my handiwork; wholly and entirely untroubled by guilt.

Chapter 21

I remember it as though it were yesterday. School was over, the firemen were on strike and it was the exact same day the Queen had her first grandson christened – Mum was, of course, totally agog at that bit of news.

It was 22nd December 1977 – a little under a week since I'd sabotaged the *Guzzi*. In truth, I'd wondered why it had taken so long for there to be any real consequences. I'd almost thought it wasn't going to happen; I'd almost forgotten what I'd done and that I'd been responsible. *Almost*.

I was watching *The Goodies* on telly with Mum when Jason left. Fittingly, it was the episode when the whole world explodes at the end. I can't remember much more about the story but it was set on Christmas Eve and it was the one in which Bill had bought a skateboard and Graeme had bought a 'skateboard destruction kit' that consisted of a gun, a hammer and a bomb with a detonator and I'd thought that was the funniest thing I'd ever seen. I remember rolling around on the floor laughing uncontrollably until my guts ached and Mum asked – with genuine concern – if I was feeling alright. I also remember Tim Brooke-Taylor wearing a placard saying "The End Of The World Is Nigh". Little did I know that was just how I'd be feeling only a few hours later.

I'd gone to bed pretty late by normal standards. Even on weekends, when it was term time, I had to be in bed by midnight. However, when it was the holidays, Mum let me stay up watching late night TV and I sometimes went to bed after she did. That night was a case in point. Mum had taken herself off to bed with a book she wanted to read – some Jackie Collins thing. "They're trash but everyone reads them," she said to me once by way of apology. Jason said people only read them "for the dirty bits" – which temporarily stoked my interest – but they weren't quite as accessible to me as the magazines stashed in Jason's room.

I felt it was my lucky night when a *Hammer* horror movie came on TV. They always had horror films on telly at Christmas – I wasn't sure why but it was something you could definitely rely on. This was one of the best ones – *Dracula, Prince Of Darkness* – the one where Dracula was brought back to life by his evil butler, Klove, cutting the throat of an unsuspecting traveller who'd been marooned at Castle Dracula. I fetched myself a bag of crisps and a bottle of *Panda Pop* from the kitchen and settled down happily.

It must have been nearly 1am when the film ended. Jason still wasn't back – which wasn't necessarily unusual. I figured he was probably staying over with Cherry. I crept upstairs, quiet as a burglar. The light was off in Mum's room. If I'd been half an hour earlier I'd probably have glimpsed her through the partly open door, propped against two pillows, reading her book with the aid of an angle-poise lamp.

I tip-toed carefully into the bathroom. I hadn't planned to brush my teeth but I found myself feeling too guilty not to do it as it was one of the conditions Mum had levied on me to allow me to stay up and watch the movie: "Get in your jim-jams and clean your teeth before you get into bed," she'd instructed. "And clean both of your teeth!" she'd added – it was one of her favourite jokes. I had to be careful not to wake her so I didn't put the bathroom light on. Luckily, there was just enough moonlight to see what I was doing.

A few minutes later, I sat on my bed looking at the space I'd cleared for my new fish tank. Only three days to go, I told myself. If Jason killed these fish, I'd do more than just damage his *Guzzi*. I climbed beneath the covers feeling a surge of anger once more. The feeling ebbed and flowed but it had never totally left me.

The other day, I'd retrieved my dirty dressing gown from beneath the bed and taken it down the street to a rubbish bin. The file, still wrapped in a T-shirt, suffered the same fate but using a different litter bin. I felt I'd covered my tracks pretty well – like a criminal mastermind. Now, if anything happened, there'd be no evidence to connect me to the nobbled *Guzzi*.

Sleep came quickly but it didn't last long. I was in the complete darkness of a dreamless sleep when I felt my mother shaking me awake. I stared at her blankly a few times, unsure if this was reality, as she gradually swam into my consciousness.

"Wake up, Robin! Wake up!" Mum yelled as she shook me. "Robin, wake up!"

I didn't want to say anything in case this actually *was* a dream. I didn't want to call out in my sleep and look stupid so I just stared dumbly at her. Her hair was a mess and she was half dressed. She looked panicked.

"Robin, there's been an accident. It's Jason. He's in hospital. Robin, for God's sake, wake up."

"What?" I eventually stammered.

"It's Jason. There's been a crash. He's in the West Middlesex Hospital. Get dressed. I'll explain on the way."

And, with that, she was gone – back into her own room to finish getting dressed.

I put the bedside light on and sat on the bed, my head spinning. So, Jason had crashed. I didn't know whether to feel horrified or elated – so I ended up feeling both at the same time. It was clearly my fault – which gave me both a sense of power and a sense of dread. I didn't know what to feel and I didn't know what to think – I just sat there staring stupidly into the harsh electric light. I don't know how much time passed before Mum poked her head round my bedroom door again. This time she was fully dressed and even had her coat on.

"Come on, Robin. Get moving. Don't just sit there. There's a minicab coming. It'll be here any minute. We've got to see your brother. Come on, move!"

I sat like a statue. A new feeling had swept over me – guilt. The feeling made me cold and clammy and nauseous. I thought I might throw up. It was accompanied by a wave of fear – fear of discovery and fear of retribution. I wasn't going anywhere. Mum misinterpreted my inaction as shock. She changed her tactics, walked over, sat next to me, put both her arms around me and held me tightly.

"I know it's a shock, love," she said. "It's a shock for me too. But he's going to be alright – the doctors told me. They said it's bad but he's going to be okay."

She wasn't making any sense. I looked at her blankly but said nothing. She carried on babbling – half reassuring me, half reassuring herself.

"The hospital called. I was asleep. They had to repeat it three or four times. He's alive. It's bad but he'll live. We've got to go. We've got to see him. Come on, love."

"You go," I said eventually. "I'll stay here."

"What? What are you talking about? Robin, you're not making any sense."

"You go," I repeated. "I'll be fine here."

As if the news about Jason's crash hadn't been shocking enough, now Mum looked totally floored by my refusal to move. She stared at me open-mouthed for what seemed an age. She couldn't understand where I was coming from and, I reflected, that was probably just as well. Once again, she generously attributed my static response to shock. She began to speak to me very slowly – as if addressing a foreigner with only very little English.

"Robin, your brother is in hospital. He nearly died but he's going to be okay; he's alive. We – *both* of us – have to go and see him. Now. We're going now. Robin, it will be okay. He will live. Come on, love. Get yourself ready. He'll be okay, I promise."

Car headlights swept across the curtains. Mum dashed across to the window and peered out.

"The minicab's here. Now, come on Robin, get dressed. I'll tell the driver five minutes."

Then she was gone – leaving me with a toxic cocktail of mixed feelings. Slowly, I went to my cupboard and pulled out random items – a checked shirt, my woollen school jumper, dark blue jeans. I was hopping round the room with one leg in the jeans when Mum reappeared.

"Five minutes," she said, watching me struggle to dress myself. "Come on. We need to find out what happened. We need to see if Cherry's okay too."

I stopped dead, an icy shiver pervading my entire being.

"Cherry was with him?" I gulped, incredulously.

"Yes, of course," Mum answered, as though I were stupid. "They're both in the hospital together. They wouldn't give me any details about her, though. Family only, they said."

Cherry! My God, what have I done? I'd never – not for one single second – considered that Cherry might have somehow been affected by my rash actions. Now I had to get to the hospital right away. I had to be at Cherry's bedside more than I had to be anywhere else on earth. I had to see if *she* was okay.

I was dressed in seconds and Mum found herself following *me* out of the house.

Chapter 22

The hospital smelled funny – hospitals always do. It was a sickly sweet smell mixed with industrial bleach and plastic – hard to describe but only hospitals ever smelled quite like that. The smell was pervasive and there was no getting away from it – it was on every floor, in every corridor, in every ward, in every room.

To me, it was the unavoidable smell of my own guilt. It was, for me, a supernatural stench that was pointing its vaporous finger at me; it clung to me and I felt it would never go away.

The smell followed us as we searched the hospital in an effort to locate Jason. Mum had asked for him at the front desk but neither of us really took in what the woman had said. Something about the 'Isleworth Ward'. We went up some stairs, along a corridor, trying to follow fading signs that didn't seem to make sense. Hospital paraphernalia impeded our progress – trolleys, wheelchairs, weird contraptions on wheels that had wires coming out of them and looked like they belonged in Mum's hair salon rather than a hospital. We hit a dead end more than once.

"This is ridiculous," Mum snarled, before launching into a coughing fit. "We'll never find him at this rate. He could be dead by now!"

I tried to calm her but she wasn't listening. A passing nurse took pity on us. I explained why we were there – while Mum tried to stifle her cough.

"I'm gasping for a fag," Mum joked with the nurse as she lead us to Jason's room. It was on the floor directly above us.

The nurse left us in the presence of a doctor. You could tell it was a doctor because he wore a white coat and carried a stethoscope. Apparently he'd been waiting for us. He'd posted himself outside Jason's room. It seemed he wanted to talk to Mum and explain Jason's injuries before we saw him. The doctor looked at me – he was quite old and completely bald except for a small white moustache that made him look a bit like Alf Garnett.

"You might want to take a seat over there, lad," the doctor said to me, indicating some plastic chairs of the type we used for school assembly. I started to walk away numbly. However, Mum caught me by the shoulder and pulled me back.

"No, this is Jason's brother. He stays. Anything you need to say to me you can say to him too."

She gripped my shoulders tightly – to the point it almost hurt. I think she wanted me there as much for the support I provided to her as for the opportunity for me to hear about my brother. If I hadn't been there, Mum just might have fallen over; certainly she'd have needed to sit down.

"Very well," the doctor said uncertainly, looking warily at me again. To me, it was as if he could actually see guilt pouring off me like a toxic river. I squirmed uncomfortably but Mum just gripped me tighter.

"Your son is lucky to be alive," the doctor continued. "In fact, if it wasn't for his crash helmet, he wouldn't be here; he'd be in the morgue. The good news, however, is that he will definitely live. He's not in a great condition at the moment but we'll move him to the main ward as soon as we can. For now, he's in a private room."

"Oh my God," Mum wailed. I felt like wailing too but, in my case, it was guilt not sorrow. I never intended things to turn out this badly.

The doctor placed an arm on Mum's shoulders and looked her in the eyes.

"As I said, Mrs Bellamy, Jason *will* live. But his injuries are quite extensive. He has six broken ribs and a punctured lung. There's also some concern as to the extent of the spinal damage he's suffered. To be blunt, Mrs Bellamy, we're not sure yet if Jason will be able to walk again."

I nearly laughed hysterically at this announcement. Even in my distress (at my own guilt, not Jason's suffering) this seemed a deliciously ironic outcome. Almost as a distraction, I grabbed hold of the doctor's white coat and pulled it – the action of a small child trying to get a parent's attention.

"What about Cherry?" I blurted.

The doctor looked at me, puzzled. Mum rescued the situation.

"I'm sorry, doctor. Cherry – the girl who was with Jason on the motorbike; Jason's girlfriend."

The doctor nodded, all of a sudden in the picture.

"I'm afraid Cherry has sustained serious injuries too. Pierced bladder, broken pelvis. We're concerned about her walking as well. She'll live too, though, I'm very pleased to say."

At this point, it was all too much. I broke away from Mum, walked over to the wall and started hitting and kicking it, before bashing my head against it quite hard. Mum and the doctor prised me away and sat me down on one of the nearby plastic chairs.

"I did try to tell you this in private, Mrs Bellamy," I heard the doctor mutter under his breath.

"Robin, Robin – it's going to be okay. They're both going to live. Do you hear me? They are both going to live."

She sounded like she was convincing herself as much as me.

"Can we see her?" I blurted.

"What?" Mum couldn't believe my only concern seemed to be Cherry.

"Can we see her?" I repeated, now shouting it out.

How stupid was Mum? Didn't she realise I needed to see Cherry? I had to tell Cherry I was sorry. I had to make amends. I couldn't vocalise it but I sure as heck felt it.

"I'll leave you both alone for a while," the doctor said to Mum. "Feel free to see your son when you're ready. My room is just along there on the right if you need me. Feel free to ask me anything you need to."

The doctor wandered off leaving Mum staring at me with utter incredulity.

"You want to see *her* but *not* your own brother?" Mum asked angrily.

"It's not a competition, is it?" I snapped back.

"I know you're keen on her, Robin," Mum said. "But don't you want to see your own brother?"

"It's not that," I protested.

In fact, it was *exactly* that. He'd *know* what I'd done and I didn't want to face him and be exposed for what I'd done in front of my mother. Plus, I felt sorry for what had happened to Cherry. I didn't feel sorry for what had happened to Jason; in truth, for a time, I'd even exulted in it. I was glad Jason hadn't actually been killed but he'd had this coming. It was payback for every year of shit I'd endured at his hands – and boots. At last the worm had turned and the worm had discovered it owned teeth! Of course, I couldn't tell my mother any of *that*. I had to think of an explanation quickly though – I could see how it looked otherwise.

"I…I don't want to see him like *that*," I lied. Actually, that was partly true. "I want to see him when he's well, when he's okay; not when he's all smashed up and broken."

This gave Mum pause for thought. She considered my reasoning briefly and then, all at once, her sympathetic demeanour returned. She seemed convinced I didn't want to see my 'idolised' older brother looking vulnerable and weak. Just as I'd hoped, Mum had concluded it was some sort of little brother/big brother 'thing'. Mum put a hand behind my head and stroked my neck tenderly.

"Come on, lovey, it'll be okay," she coaxed. "I'll be with you. We'll go in together. Come on."

There was no way out of it. I'd simply have to go in and face the music. My life as I knew it was about to end. Just as it had seemed I'd gained the ultimate revenge on Jason, he was about to visit the ultimate humiliation on me that would see me ending up being hated by both my mother *and* Cherry for evermore. Well, if that was going to happen, it was going to happen – I might as well just grit my teeth and get it over with. I stood up and held Mum's hand tightly as we advanced towards the door of Jason's hospital bedroom.

Chapter 23

Jason looked tiny and vulnerable and not at all scary lying in his hospital bed. It was difficult to believe it was actually him. Somehow he seemed even smaller than me.

I knew it was an illusion but it still took me aback. It emboldened me even as it horrified me. Jason was hooked up to some contraption that bleeped occasionally. However, the most noticeable thing was the surgical strapping they'd wrapped all around his torso – no doubt to protect his ribs and help him to breathe. He was propped against some hard padded board they'd placed at his back so he was sitting almost upright, the bedclothes starting at the top of his hips, the rest of him out in the open.

"Fucking hell," he cackled on seeing the pair of us enter the room. Some things never change, I thought. "Look what the cat just dragged in. Sorry to get you out of bed, Mum."

At this Mum burst into tears and rushed over to him.

"Watch out, watch out!" he cautioned. "It hurts like fuck being touched!"

Mum pulled back. Her instinct had been to hug him. Instead, she sat in the chair by the bed and took his left hand in both of hers and kissed it – like she was meeting Jesus or something. I wondered if I could edge out of the room backwards and, if I did, whether either of them would notice. As Mum wordlessly clasped Jason's hand to her cheek, he caught my eye with a steely gaze. I froze on the spot, hardly daring to breathe.

"Oi, LB, come here you ugly little tit!" Like I said, some things never change. "Come on, I won't bite…well, maybe!"

I edged nervously towards the bed and stood behind Mum, out of his reach. Objectively, I knew he was in no fit state to do anything to me but, psychologically, keeping anything other than a safe distance from Jason was a tough habit to break.

"What happened?" I said. I couldn't think of anything else to say.

Suddenly Jason began to laugh – at first they were small convulsions of mirth then he unleashed great sobbing howls of laughter that made the whole bed shake. The laughter was punctuated by cries of pain as the shaking affected his broken ribs and punctured lung.

"Ow, ow, it hurts to laugh, ow, shit, ow. What a stupid fucking question! That's the stupidest question I've ever heard in my entire fucking life!"

Now the laughter returned and it was so infectious Mum started laughing too and then even I was laughing (even though I was the butt of the joke and I didn't quite understand what I was actually laughing at). It was probably the ice breaker we all needed though. All three of us had tears streaming from our eyes. Jason was the first to recover. He composed himself, looked at me steadily once again and solemnly proclaimed: "What happened is…I crashed." And then the laughter began all over again.

I went round to the far side of his bed and stood there. Jason even let me hold his other hand – he stuck it out for me and waved his fingers until I gripped on. So there we were – me on one side, Mum on the other and Jason in the middle having a hand held by each of us. I don't know how long we stayed like that but it was long enough for my legs to start aching.

Mostly Mum and Jason talked and I just listened. I occasionally chipped in but only when I was asked a question and, even then, I remained as monosyllabic as possible.

I was petrified in case Jason confronted me over my sabotage of the *Guzzi* and terrified in case he should reveal my crime right there and then while I was holding his hand and Mum was weeping at his bedside. I felt like the worst kind of Judas. But the longer they talked, the more I thought I might have got away with it. Could it really be possible he hadn't noticed what I'd done?

I listened carefully – rapt with attention and apparent brotherly concern – as Jason told Mum he remembered nothing about the crash beyond the fact they were cresting a small hill and then he woke in hospital in pain, finding it hard to breathe. It seemed a long time before Jason asked after Cherry's well-being. If it was me, the first thing I would have asked about would have been whether Cherry was okay. When Jason finally enquired, it seemed to be almost a casual afterthought.

"How's Cherry?" he asked Mum, almost as a polite enquiry and certainly not in the tone you'd expect when Cherry's life might have been hanging in the balance.

"She's going to be okay, love. The doctor said as much. That's the main thing. We haven't seen her yet, though. We both came straight here to see you first."

"I want to see her," I blurted out. I couldn't stop myself sounding desperate. They both looked at me, slightly stunned. "What?" I said defensively.

Jason smiled. It was seemingly indulgent rather than sinister, which somehow disturbed me even more.

"That's right, LB. You go and see her for me. Tell me how she is. See if she's still speaking to me."

"She can't blame you." Mum said. "It was an accident."

"If you say so," Jason replied enigmatically.

I couldn't help but let his hand drop the moment he said that.

"What do you mean?" Mum asked, a new note of concern in her voice. "It *was* an *accident*, wasn't it?"

Jason waved his hand for me to take hold of it again. I found the gesture deeply worrying – was he *now* going to reveal all and dump me in it at the eleventh hour? I grasped his hand like a condemned man.

"Of course it was an accident," Jason continued. At that moment I could have kissed him! "But she might not see it like that, might she? And I'm sure as hell certain her old man won't see it that way."

"Oh my God, of course," Mum said. "I hadn't thought of that."

The point was left hanging in the air and it took me a moment to work out what they meant. Then it dawned on me. Cherry's Mum had died and Cherry was all her Dad had left. She had no brothers or sisters. If she died, her Dad was all alone. If she died and Jason was to blame, Cherry's Dad would probably kill him.

"He'll understand," Mum continued.

"Will he?" Jason asked, one eyebrow raised quizzically.

"I'll tell him," Mum offered.

"He's not the kind of guy who listens to reason." Jason countered. "Least of all over something like this. I think we're finished, she and I."

It was the first time I'd ever seen Jason appear scared of anyone or anything.

"I'll tell him," Mum repeated.

"And I'll go and see her, like you want," I offered.

Suddenly I was the solicitous, concerned little brother for real. Not only did I actually want to help him – to atone as best I could for my prior sins – but I also realised it was the only way I could still keep Cherry in my life as well. Jason actually squeezed my hand with a semblance of affection.

"You're not a complete tit, LB, are you?" he cackled. I smiled weakly.

"You need to rest, love," Mum said to him, getting to her feet. "We'll be back in the morning."

"No, wait," Jason said with some urgency. "Before you go, I'd like to talk to LB on his own for a while, if that's okay? You know, brother-to-brother."

Mum pulled a face as though she didn't actually know but she didn't want to flout Jason's wishes at a time like this.

"Well, okay," Mum said uncertainly. "But don't be too long, will you – you need to get some rest, lovey. Robin, I'm going to speak to the doctor again. You know where his room is?" I nodded. "Come and find me there. Five minutes – no longer."

I watched as Mum left us. It was the moment I'd been dreading. It felt about five thousand times worse than being called to the Headmaster's study.

Chapter 24

I stood close by the door after Mum had left, staring uncertainly at Jason as though he might suddenly fly from his bed and seize me by the throat. My demeanour seemed to amuse him.

He smiled oddly and winked at me. It was one of those winks where you slightly incline your head at the same time as you're winking; the sort of wink that silently implies you're somehow sharing a secret. He did it a couple of times. Unconsciously I edged a few steps backwards until the small of my back was pressed flat against the door.

"Come and sit beside me," Jason said at last. "Like I said before, I won't bite."

I remained plastered against the door. Jason flicked his eyes towards the empty chair at his bedside.

"Come on, don't fuck about, LB. We need to talk. Take a seat, will you."

There was no escape. If he knew, he knew. This had to happen at some point, I figured. I prised myself from the door and sidled to the chair. Jason watched, snake-like, as I lowered myself into the seat beside him. Once I'd settled, he nodded with satisfaction.

"I know it was you," he said. The words nearly cut me in two.

"What?"

It was the only response I could muster. It was just a single word but it smacked of guilt, desperation and betrayal. Jason laughed – a long, hollow, scary laugh.

"I *know* what you did," he said eventually.

I began to rise.

"Sit down!" Jason barked.

I complied. This was hell, sheer hell. I wanted to throw myself across his bed and beg for forgiveness. I wanted to die. I wondered if the window would open far enough for me to throw myself out. I felt all of these things but sat motionless; paralysed and silent.

"I *know* what you did," Jason repeated. "And I don't blame you. In fact, I admire you for it. I didn't know you had it in you, you little gobshite!"

This was a new development. I hadn't expected *that*. What was I to make of that proclamation? Jason was praising me for putting him – and Cherry (my God, *Cherry*!) – in a hospital bed? How did that make any kind of sense? Jason seemed to enjoy my puzzlement and discomfort.

"Relax," he said eventually. "It wasn't your meddling that caused the crash. It was my shitty bike control. I was cresting a hill too fast. I know you fucked with the *Guzzi* though. I saw you from the window that night and I checked the *Guzzi* over in the morning. The damage you did was superficial. I patched it up at the workshop the next morning."

"But…"

"But why didn't I kill you?"

"Well…er…yes." None of this was making any kind of sense.

Jason stared at the ceiling and let out an imaginary stream of smoke that came out as a kind of elongated whistle. It reminded me of the time he'd been lying on his back in his bedroom, telling me the legend of Jimmy Dean's car.

"Oh, I thought about it alright. I thought about giving you the hiding of your life, LB. Then I thought about everything I've ever done to you to drive you to go *that* far just to try to get back at me. I saw how far I'd pushed you and for how long. I saw that I'd finally – *finally* – made you snap. In one moment I saw everything I'd ever done to you to *make* you to act like that and I saw that I was to blame, not you."

I opened my mouth to say something but Jason silenced me, holding up his hand like a traffic cop. He was determined to finish without any interruption.

"And, frankly, LB, I admired you for finally fighting back – even if you couldn't do it with your fists. I realised it was the very same thing I would have done if our places had been reversed. To be honest, LB, I finally saw there was actually something of *me* in *you*. I finally felt *related* to you. I finally felt we were truly *brothers*. And so I decided to give you a free pass – because of *that*."

It was quite a speech. I couldn't take it all in all at once. I didn't know whether to believe him. Could I really take this Road To Damascus epiphany at face value? Or was it just another Jason-style mind game?

"I don't know what to say," I squeaked. And it was true; I absolutely didn't have the first clue how to respond.

"I bet you don't," Jason said, throwing his head back and wincing at the pain from his punctured lung and broken ribs. The longer he talked, the more wheezy his voice was becoming. He closed his eyes. Then, opening them suddenly, Jason whispered: "Come here, LB."

"What?" I blurted stupidly.

"Come here. Bring your ear closer. I'm losing my voice and there's something I need to tell you before Mum comes back."

I looked at him blankly. No way was I going to risk placing my ear in biting distance. Suddenly it was all crystal clear – the apparent brotherly concern was just a cynical ploy to win over my trust. Once my ear was near enough, he'd bite it off.

"Come on, you fool," Jason coaxed. "This is important. I need to tell you something."

It was a killer combination – guilt and curiosity. I didn't trust Jason but I felt I had to hear what he wanted to say – partly because I owed him and partly because I was dying to know what it was he wished to confide only to me.

I leaned gingerly over the bed, being careful not to put any weight on his damaged torso. I craned my neck to hold my ear near Jason's mouth. I figured he couldn't make a lunge in that condition so I stood a fair chance of evading any shark-like attack. I hovered and waited.

"Closer," Jason said. No way, I thought. "Closer, you tit," Jason whispered.

I took the risk, closing my eyes and waiting for the inevitable snap of his teeth. Instead, what came was arguably worse.

"You must have wondered why I've hated you for so long," Jason began. Before I could answer, he added the fatal blow. "You're *not* my brother," he said.

I sat back down in the chair immediately; a puppet with its strings cut, a ship with no rudder. The room swam as my guts lurched. Jason was smiling at me – an evil, malevolent grin this time. I just about kept the contents of my stomach in their place.

"What…what do you mean?" I stammered.

"Exactly that," Jason croaked. His voice was returning as he seemingly regained a measure of animation purely from the venom of his remarks.

"You are *not* my brother. Not my *full* brother anyway. Think about it, LB – we're chalk and cheese; we're *nothing* like each other; we couldn't be more different if we actually tried."

I opened my mouth to speak but nothing came out.

"We might have the same mum," Jason continued, in a tone like he was explaining something glaringly obvious to a total simpleton. "But we sure as shit don't have the same *dad*."

Now I finally found my voice.

"You're lying!" I shouted.

Jason shook his head wordlessly.

"Think about it, LB. You're *nothing* like me – or Dad, for that matter."

It was true. Jason was macho, Dad was – by all accounts – macho too. I was, well, 'sensitive' is how Mum often put it. I opened my mouth to object but nothing came out. I gaped hopelessly like a landed fish. Jason pushed himself further forward to try and square up to me before collapsing back on the bed, wincing from the pain and effort of moving. He eyed me slyly to ensure he had my full attention before he continued.

"Dad left, walked out – as you know. You won't remember because you were far too young but we all live with the consequences of Dad leaving. But have you ever asked yourself *why* Dad left? Have you, LB?"

"Well," I began hesitantly. "Mum doesn't talk about it and she doesn't like anyone asking. 'Your father left and that was his choice,' is all she'll ever say."

"Yes, but, have you ever asked yourself – even in your quieter moments – what might have been *behind* it? Exactly what makes a man – a man earning decent money driving trucks with a nice bit of cash in hand from moonlighting jobs here and there – just pack his bags and piss off completely?"

"I don't know," I wailed unhappily. "Why are you asking me this? I'm sorry for what I did – *tried* to do – and I'm glad it wasn't me that put you here after all and I'm glad you're alive but I don't see what all this stuff about Dad has got to do with…"

"Oh, *don't* you?" Jason sneered. "Dad left because of *you!*"

If I hadn't been sitting down I might have fallen over with shock.

"What the hell are you talking about?"

"Come on, LB, you're not stupid. We're nothing alike, you and I – and not long after you appear on the scene, Dad packs his bags and fucks off. Do the Maths, dumbo. But if you still can't figure out why, then I'll tell you: life was pretty good for Dad with just Mum and me and then *you* turn up, you ugly little twat. But why should *that* be a problem? Now Dad has two kids and that's great, isn't it? Only it isn't great because only *one* of them is actually *his* kid – that's me, by the way. You – some weird little poofter that doesn't even look like him, certainly doesn't think like him, isn't remotely interested in the things he and I are interested in – are just a reminder to him every single day of his existence that Mum had an *affair*. He's the sucker bringing home the bacon to bring up some other bloke's kid. There's a cuckoo in the nest and that cuckoo, LB, is *you*."

"That's bollocks! You're nuts!"

Even as I said it, the uncertain tone in my voice betrayed a dark suspicion that Jason might just be telling the truth – for once in his life.

"Am I? Well, then. Ask Mum – if you dare!"

Jason lay there and closed his eyes – a clear signal the conversation was *over*. A smug grin played across his lips.

"You're talking *shit*!" I yelled at him, standing up. "You're a *cunt*! I wish you *had* died!"

I would never have dared talk to Jason like that before – now, however, with him confined to a hospital bed and with the fire of outrage coursing through my veins, it was all I could do to stop myself attacking him physically as well as verbally.

Jason's eyes remained calmly closed, the triumphant smile fixed in place.

"Ask her," Jason said coolly. "If you've got the balls. *Then* come back and see me."

Chapter 25

I found Mum in the doctor's room exactly as she'd promised. The door had been left open as they talked – presumably so I could see them and wouldn't be left to wander the corridors like a lost sheep. I could hardly bring myself to look at her. Could what Jason had said really be *true*?

Mum looked over as I appeared in the doorway. She held up a hand, fingers splayed to indicate she needed another five minutes with the doctor. I nodded. I didn't want to be in there with her at that moment anyway.

I sat numbly on one of the chairs that lined the corridor. From there I could still see her and she could still see me. My mind was spinning. It was still the early hours of the morning. None of this seemed real. Maybe it was just a hideous nightmare. Maybe I'd wake up soon. I'd be at home – and so would Jason. There wouldn't have been any accident. Maybe my fish weren't even dead. I couldn't tell what was real anymore.

Suddenly I was aware of a man standing over me. He was tall and burly with tattoos on his Popeye forearms. He had a young man's body but an old man's features. He had a lined face with pronounced crease marks around the mouth and balding, greasy, greyish hair. He looked somehow familiar but I was fairly sure he wasn't hospital staff. The porters wore uniforms and were, frankly, cleaner-looking.

"You must be Robin," he said.

The man's voice was practically a growl and not especially

friendly. Things were getting weirder by the minute. I stared at him blankly, not speaking. In fact, I dared not speak. Now I really did believe this was all some sort of hallucination.

"I'm Cherry's dad," the man said.

Cherry! Now I had something else to worry about. How could I have forgotten about Cherry – even if temporarily? All this stuff about Mum and Dad and Jason's spiteful revelation paled into total insignificance beside my rekindled concern for Cherry. After all, Cherry might be even more badly hurt than Jason. She might even be dead!

I suddenly felt so overwhelmed I just stood up and burst into tears and threw my arms around this strange man. I stood there hugging him, crying buckets of tears into his fat belly. He smelled of sweat and beer and cigarettes. Oddly that wasn't too unpleasant – it was just unusual; somehow even more manly than Jason's cigarette-stained odour – and there was a sort of fascination in that unknown uber-masculine smell.

Cherry's Dad didn't know what to do. He allowed me to hug him and blub into his guts. He stood there awkwardly holding his hands in the air as if to demonstrate he wasn't encouraging this whole emotional carry-on in any way.

At last, Mum must have noticed me clinging to some strange man in the corridor. She shot out of the doctor's room and yelled at us both.

"What the hell is going on here?"

I'm not sure if I broke away or if Cherry's Dad pushed me away or if it was a simultaneous de-coupling but I was suddenly backing away from him in a split second. Hardly had that happened than Cherry's Dad rounded on Mum.

"Where's that other bastard son of yours?" he shouted. "If he's not dead already, I'll kill him!"

He looked as if he could overpower Jason pretty easily and he definitely looked as though he meant it.

"Back off, Tony!" Mum screamed back at him. "It takes two to ride a motorbike, you know. How do you know it was Jason's fault? Your daughter might have put her foot down at the wrong moment.

She might have overbalanced it. It could be *her* fault for all we know."

So, Cherry's Dad's name was Tony – well, that was news to me. Mum's logic seemed to stall Tony in his tracks – momentarily at least. Then his face creased into a new grimace and he made a fist that he raised ominously. Suddenly I feared for Mum. Would I have to step in somehow? What could I do? The guy looked about eight feet tall and twice as wide. Now the doctor came out of his office and stood between the two warring parents.

"Please. Sir, Madam. Calm yourselves. This is a hospital. Sir, calm yourself or I'll have you removed."

Tony turned away, placed his face in his hands briefly and then turned back. Now he spread his palms before him, face down – a gesture of conciliation.

"Okay, okay, I'm calm," he growled.

I wasn't so sure. He looked hair-trigger violent – even more so than Jason, if that were possible. Mum stood her ground like a terrier. I'd never been as proud of her. But the situation was awful. The last thing I wanted was open warfare between my family and Cherry's family. That was horrendous, horrific; way beyond awful.

"Can I see her please?" I pleaded, tugging at Tony's t-shirt.

That seemed to break the ice between the two combatants. Tony stood looking aghast at my new display of heightened emotion.

"Can he, Tony?" Mum asked. "He loves her, you know. Like a sister."

I was so glad Mum added that final sentence. The last thing I wanted was to be revealed as lusting after the man's daughter in the middle of the hospital. But I *did* love her, that part was certainly true. To my astonishment, Tony suddenly burst into floods of tears, crying like a baby, holding his eyes with his fingers as if to keep the misery at bay.

"I thought I'd lost her, Rose," he blubbed. "She's my only daughter, my only child. After her mother died…well…and now… this happens…"

Mum stepped forward and suddenly she was hugging Tony, consoling him as best she could. I noticed she couldn't close her arms completely around him. He looked like a professional wrestler. Big Daddy. Giant Haystacks. Kendo Nagasaki. One of those sorts anyway. The doctor stood nearby, an uncomfortable rictus grin trying to convey his blessing upon the two previously sparring adults now virtually kissing and making up.

"Take the boy to see her, Tony," Mum counselled. "Honestly, he's been as worried for Cherry as he is for Jason. More so, perhaps."

I was now apparently 'the boy' rather than 'Robin'. I also detected the implied criticism in her comment – although it seemed Tony did not. Tony kissed the top of Mum's head – it was an odd gesture, I thought.

"Yes, yes, I will," he said.

He looked directly at the doctor, as if seeking his permission. The doctor nodded.

"Come on, lad," Tony said, grabbing me by the hand and dragging me away.

"I'll be right here, Robin," Mum called, sitting in the chair I had so recently occupied.

Tony's grip was like a vice. I hoped Cherry's room wasn't too far away or my fingers might be broken by the time we got there and then I'd be needing the hospital's services too.

Chapter 26

Cherry's room looked exactly the same as Jason's – except for a solitary vase of flowers by the bed; a nod to her femininity, I supposed. Cherry didn't seem to notice us enter the room so we tip-toed across to her bed, still holding hands.

As we hovered over her, side by side like emissaries, Tony at last let go of my hand. I resisted the temptation to shake some life back into my fingers and quickly plunged the crushed hand into my pocket instead. Cherry's eyes were closed. Tony reached out and touched her cheek with a soft caress.

"Princess," he said quietly. "I'm here, Princess." Then, seemingly an afterthought, he added: "And Robin's here too."

For one horrific moment I thought she might be dead. The rising sense of panic within me was overwhelming and I thought I would faint. I felt myself going all woozy. At that very instant, Cherry's eyes flickered and opened. I could see her struggling for focus.

Like Jason, she looked much smaller in her hospital bed – like a child somehow. Cherry's face had light purple bruises and there were several darker bruises up her forearms. There was a tube trailing out from under the bedclothes on the far side of her bed that seemed to be coming directly from Cherry's body.

Tony later told me it was called a catheter. He added that she'd broken her pelvis in three places and she'd have to stay flat on her back in hospital for at least six weeks. That also explained the over-sized pillows cocooning her in the bed so she couldn't move. Her muscles were bound to waste, Tony said. She'd have to learn to walk again from scratch – if she could walk again at all. It was too awful to contemplate.

"Robin?" It was as if she didn't believe I was real. She said it as if in a dream.

I was secretly thrilled Cherry had focused on me ahead of her own father, even though he was standing right there.

"Robin?" Cherry repeated. I sat there dumbly, smiling weakly.

"I'm here Princess," said Tony, more assertively this time – as though staking a claim to his property.

"Dad?" she enquired.

I began to think she'd lost her marbles and I started to panic once more. Cherry was never going to be the same again. She'd never be back in our house visiting either me or Jason.

"Don't try to move, love," said Tony as Cherry strained to sit up. "The doctors said you've got to stay put. You'll damage yourself if you try to move."

"It was an accident, Dad." Cherry said suddenly.

"I know it was, love," Tony whispered cooingly at her. His statement seemed pretty unconvincing to me, let alone to Cherry.

"You can't blame Jason," Cherry insisted. "It wasn't his fault. It was an *accident*."

"I know," said Tony. Now he sounded grudging.

I couldn't ignore the contrast. Jason had barely mentioned Cherry but practically the first thing Cherry did on waking was not only to speak about Jason but also to attempt to absolve him of any blame in front of her scary Dad. Now I felt an overwhelming urge to speak.

"He asked about you, Cherry," I blurted. "Jason. The first thing he did on waking was ask 'how's Cherry?' The very first thing…"

I looked uncertainly at Cherry's dad. Now I sounded just as unconvincing as him. Cherry seemed to be pleased with the lie, though. She smiled and looked at me – her eyes focusing much more clearly this time.

"Did he, Robin? That's nice. Is he going to be okay? Is he badly hurt? Is he…?"

"Don't you worry about him," Tony grunted. "He's better off

than you are."

"Anyone's better off than I am right now," Cherry chuckled.

"You'll be home before you know it, Princess," Tony continued. "You just concentrate on getting well."

"Can I see him?" Cherry asked.

Tony was probably tempted to ask 'who?' but neither of us said anything in reply.

"Will you give him a message for me, Robin?"

"Yes, yes, anything," I said eagerly.

"Tell him I love him," she said and then she closed her eyes and, it seemed, went straight to sleep or simply lost consciousness. I didn't even have time to reply.

"I love you, Cherry," I said and promptly burst into tears.

Tony was on his feet and in the corridor in an instant, yelling for a doctor. We both thought she might be dying but our reactions were totally different. I just sat there feeling sorry for myself as well as for her. Tony, though, was a man of action. It was just as well he'd left the room because he didn't hear me blaming myself for everything that had happened, confessing to the sleeping, unconscious (or dead?) Cherry everything I believed had led her to a hospital bed.

"I'm so very sorry Cherry," I mumbled. "I didn't mean to do it. I didn't mean to hurt you. I wanted to hurt him. It was *him*, not *you*. I'd never hurt you. Not in a million years. Not ever. I love you, Cherry. Please, Cherry, forgive me. Please, Cherry, don't die. Please Cherry, don't die…"

Tony returned with a doctor – one I hadn't seen before (who looked a bit like a mad professor with wispy flyaway hair) – and they both entered the room to hear me muttering 'don't die…don't die' over and over but, thankfully, caught none of the rest of my rabid confessions.

The doctor moved me firmly aside with his hand and I stood with Tony as he examined Cherry. The silent examination seemed to go on forever while Tony and I stood like statues, white as the hospital sheets. The doctor fussed over Cherry, checked the bleeping electronic equipment to which she was attached. Then he fussed over Cherry once more and finally turned to face us. When he spoke, he spoke directly to Tony – as if I were completely invisible.

"She's resting. She's going to be alright. She's likely to drift in and out of consciousness like this for quite some time yet. That's normal – the accident was a major shock to her system. Physically, she's ok, though, let me assure you. But we do need to monitor her brain activity – that's why she's in a private room. We'll move her to the ward once we're sure she's okay in that regard. Physically, she's fine – once again, please let me to reassure you of that. Best let her get some rest for now. You and your son can come back and visit her tomorrow." He smiled benignly with practised professionalism.

Neither Tony or I acknowledged the doctor's remark about me being Tony's son.

"Come on," Tony said to me gruffly – but not wholly without affection – "let's get you back to your mother."

Chapter 27

"Let's get the bus home," Mum said. "I can't afford a mini-cab two ways."

She motioned to take me by the hand but I pulled away. Mum looked at me quizzically. I didn't have the heart to explain my sudden rejection of her. I felt terrible believing Jason and his stupid lies but I couldn't shake what he'd said from my mind and, as a result, I didn't want to be around Mum just at that moment. However, Mum wasn't too concerned about pursuing an explanation for my odd behaviour. Most likely she put it down to tiredness or the fact a sudden shock does strange things to people.

"Come on, Robin, let's go home." Mum said softly.

She said it so kindly and with such obvious concern that I burst into tears. It was hard to explain but I didn't want Mum being all nice and caring and comforting towards me. It didn't fit with the image of the harridan, harlot and betrayer that Jason had just painted. It didn't fit with the guilt I felt at my own sly actions in attempting to sabotage the *Guzzi* either.

It was all too confusing. Jason and Cherry had almost died. Was it my fault or wasn't it? Was Jason making it up about knowing of my interference with the *Guzzi*? Was I *really* off the hook for the crash? But how could Jason have known what I did to his motorbike if he *hadn't* actually seen me from the window? Maybe he just *guessed* what I'd done? No, he wasn't that smart – I could rely on that much being true. And how could I possibly confront Mum about what Jason had said about her? How could I even begin to do *that*?

Mum was cradling me now as my body shook like a despairing child's. Mum held me surprisingly tightly. I didn't know she still possessed such a wiry strength – I thought all those cigarettes had damaged her. She whispered soothingly in my ear.

"He's going to be okay, love. He's going to be okay. Let's just go home."

My response was to cry even harder. Mum changed tack.

"*She's* going to be okay too, *promise*." Mum whispered.

My sobbing stopped almost immediately. Was I really that transparent?

Outside it was cold and pitch black – even though it was technically morning now. I hadn't dressed for the weather – just jumped in the minicab when it arrived. I had no coat. We reached the bus stop at 6.30am. Mum lit a match to try to read the timetable while I shivered and watched my breath curling upwards into the cold morning air like some parody of Mum's smoking.

"There's one due at 6.33 a.m," Mum said before the match blew out. "Three minutes, that's not so bad."

Once again she hugged me close. Not only to comfort me or keep me warm but also partly to keep herself warm too, I suspected.

"Buses are always late," I said gloomily, ever the pessimist.

"Not at this time of the morning," Mum countered. "It'll be the first one out of the depot. This is about the one time in the day the timetable *can* be trusted."

Happily, Mum was right. About three minutes later a twin layer of glaring yellow lights appeared in the distance, underpinned by two strong beams of white light that swept up the road towards us. Mum squinted into the distance towards the advancing lights.

"267. That's us."

She stuck her arm out and put one foot in the road. No way was the driver going to be allowed to accidently breeze past us. We went upstairs on the bus. Mum said it was so I could look out of the window but I realised it was really so she could smoke a ciggie.

The bus was completely empty. We huddled together at the rear of the top deck, near the stairs. The conductor came upstairs and fired a couple of tickets out of his crank-handled ticket machine.

"Alright love," he said to Mum, giving her a cheeky wink.

Mum smiled pleasantly and lit up the moment he'd gone.

"What a Christmas this is going to be," she sighed. "I thought the last one was bad enough."

I stared out of the window and said nothing. Christmas! Tomorrow – or, rather, the remainder of today – was Christmas Eve. The whole way home everywhere I looked had shops and houses decked with coloured lights and Santa-themed displays. I'd been in such a state I'd barely noticed the tawdry efforts at decorating the hospital. Now, tinsel covered trees glittered in endless successive house windows seeming only to make a direct mockery of my own personal misery. For a second I thought about the new fish tank I was supposed to be getting. That would probably be delayed now – if I even deserved it at all, that is. Then I thought about Mum – and Dad – and everything Jason had said. I wondered how long I could hold my silence. At least I managed it for the bus journey.

Once we arrived home I went straight to my room, shut the door and threw myself on the bed. I buried my face in the pillow. More wracking sobs came that shook the bed violently and I bit into the pillow to prevent myself crying out. It was pure unadulterated self-pity. Every drop of saline streaming from my eyes and soaking my pillow was shed solely and exclusively for me, myself, alone. How had my life become such a nightmare? Had I really done anything – besides attacking the *Guzzi* – to deserve any of this?

I cried until there was nothing left. When I'd finished, I rose from the bed and approached the mirror on the back of my bedroom door. I was both curious and wary of discovering how bad I looked after blubbing myself stupid. How puffy would my eyes be? How red? How flat and plastered to my head would my proudly spiked hair now be? Luckily, it was not as bad as I'd feared. My eyes were a bit red and the eyelids a bit puffy but my hair was still defiantly pointing daggers at the ceiling. I could now go downstairs and face Mum again.

Mum. She'd had the sense not to follow me upstairs, not to question what I was doing; just leave me alone to sort myself out. Now I'd burned myself out. Now I could face her. Or could I? Every time I looked at her – or even thought about her – I was reminded of what Jason had just said. How could I shut that out and try to compartmentalise it and stop it plaguing my psyche? I wasn't a magician; I couldn't hypnotise myself or anything like that. No, I'd just have to confront her; go and talk it over. But *how*? How can you even bring up something like *that* and with your own *mother* too? At that moment I wanted to stay in my bedroom forever – never to see Mum again, or Jason for that matter. But that really wasn't an option. Feeling every microbe like the condemned man, I opened my bedroom door and walked slowly downstairs, every step one closer to the scaffold.

Chapter 28

Mum sat at the kitchen table, her eyes as red-rimmed as mine and the inevitable cigarette burning away in an ashtray beside her. Tendrils of smoke curled upwards, threatening to discolour the paper chains, tinsel and other Christmas decorations that hung loosely around the kitchen.

The contrast between my mother's expression and the bright but tacky seasonal adornments would have been comical but for the sadness in her eyes. A flicker of hope crossed her face as I entered the room but it dissipated almost immediately as she saw my blank response.

I felt unutterably cruel but I couldn't help myself. My natural impulse had been to comfort her but Jason's allegations prevented me; they distorted my viewpoint and warped my thinking so that, try as I might, I could only see her at that precise moment as a tormentor and a betrayer – a keeper of secrets that would rock me to the core of my being and play with my very sense of my identity and my place in the world.

How could she possibly foist all of that upon me and how could I even dare to raise it as an issue? All things considered, I think I did well to retain a blank visage and not simply stare at her with undisguised hostility.

I sat opposite Mum and once more began wondering how I could say what I needed to say; how I could find a way to bring up a subject that had lain dormant and unspoken for well over a decade while using sufficient tact and diplomacy that our relationship could survive even my broaching of the issue.

Nothing came to mind and so I sat there dumbly in a steaming mess of frustration and torment as an uneasy silence reigned between us. Suddenly, Mum seemed to remember her ever-diminishing cigarette, snatched it up from the ashtray and eyed me inscrutably as she inhaled.

"Did you have a good sleep, love?" she asked. "I thought it best to leave you to catch up for a wee while."

I said nothing. What *could* I say?

"Robin, listen, we need to talk." Mum continued. "I know this has been a tremendous shock – for you, for me, for everyone. Not least for Jason and Cherry – let's not forget them in all of this. But, thank God, no one has died. Life must go on. We have to pick ourselves up and carry on as normal as best we can. After all, it's Christmas Day tomorrow."

"It's not that…" I began. Mum seemed not to hear me.

"I've asked the hospital and they've said we can visit him tomorrow. Christmas Day in hospital. That's certainly not something I've ever experienced before."

Mum laughed sardonically and stubbed out her cigarette. Without pausing for breath, she fumbled in her nearby fag packet and immediately lit up a new one.

"I don't want to go." I said, flatly.

Mum stared at me aghast, uncomprehending. The newly lit cigarette hovered between her fingers in a shaking hand and her mouth hung loosely open like one of my fish Jason had killed when all this horror began.

"What did you say?" Mum asked, her tone a blend of threat and incomprehension.

"I don't want to go." I repeated, flatly. "To hospital. Tomorrow. I don't want to go. I can't face it."

Mum slammed her palm down flat on the table, the cigarette flying out of her hand, rolling across the table top and onto the floor by my feet.

"You selfish, *selfish* little boy!" she shouted at me. "I can't believe this of you, Robin. This isn't like you. Where is this coming from all of a sudden? You should be thinking of others before yourself. There are two people we both love lying in a hospital, lucky to be alive and you're telling me you can't even be *bothered* to go and see them? For a couple of hours on *Christmas Day*, of all days? And one of them is your *own brother*!"

"But is he, though?" I muttered, stooping to retrieve Mum's cigarette for her.

"What did you say?" Mum snarled. "If you're going to say something to me then say it – don't just mumble moodily under your breath, young man."

I handed her the cigarette and she angrily stubbed it out, mashing it into the overflowing mess in the ashtray with a viciousness bordering on the scary.

"I said," I began, now wholly given over to recklessness and prepared to blurt whatever I liked regardless of all and any consequences. "He's *not* my brother, is he? Not my *full* brother anyway."

Mum sat stunned for a moment and stared at me as if unsure I was still sane. I'd taken a few careful steps back from the table for my own protection. It wouldn't have surprised me if the ashtray had come flying in my direction then – Jason-style.

"What the *hell* are you talking about?" Mum asked eventually, in a voice more bewildered than angry.

"Jason. He's not my brother. Not my *full* brother, anyway. We've not got the same father, have we? He told me that. That's what *he* told me. Exactly that. Just now. When we were alone in the hospital. Jason told me I've got a different Dad to him. Dad is not my Dad. *He* told me that. Jason. Jason said it. He said 'ask Mum'. He said: 'Ask Mum if you don't believe me'. Those were his exact words."

It all came out in a rush – a kind of 'speaking in tongues' flood. And I felt better – at least momentarily – for getting it all off my chest; for saying it out loud; for stopping it all swirling round and round inside my head. But, at the same time, I also wished I'd said nothing at all because the effect my words had on Mum were unimaginable to me. She sat silent and as still as a statue, seemingly in a kind of fugue. I had rendered her both speechless and immobile. For a second, I even wondered if she was still alive.

"Mum? Mum?" I asked uncertainly. I took a step towards her and then, fearing she might strike out suddenly, like a timorous prey animal, I took a step back again.

"Is that *really* what you think of me?" Mum eventually hissed.

I didn't know what to say. I felt like pissing in my pants. This was all too awful to comprehend. What could I say to put this *right*?

"Think what you're accusing me of, Robin." Mum said. "Think what you're *implying* by even asking this. I'm not going to dignify this with a reply."

I sat down at the table opposite her, careless now of the risk of being slapped or otherwise assaulted. I grabbed both her hands in mine. To my horror, she drew her hands away.

"But it was *him*," I wailed. "*He* said it, not me."

"But *you* believed him, didn't you? *Didn't* you, Robin? And that's why you're saying this to me now. Accusing me of all sorts."

"He said it was why he hated me. He said it was why he bullied me and beat me up all these years. He said it was because I'd driven Dad away because whenever Dad looked at me he saw another man's son and Dad couldn't stand the torment. He said..."

My mother laughed. A sharp, contemptuous sound. Catty, dismissive, frightening – a noise I would not have associated with her.

"It sounds like he said a lot of things, Robin. But you *believed* him. *That's* what hurts."

"I *didn't* believe him." I wailed in protest. "I didn't know what to think. I *still* don't."

Mum seemed to calm down then. A new cigarette was drawn from the pack and lit. She reached across the table and gave my hand a reassuring squeeze.

"It was probably the drugs talking, not him," Mum said reflectively, almost talking to herself. "They pump them full of all sorts in these hospitals – mainly to kill the pain. You don't know what the side effects might be. Jason clearly wasn't in his right mind when he put all this nonsense in your head."

Mum sat back in her chair, took a drag on the cigarette and smiled at me oddly. She exhaled slowly and then leant forward again, fixing me squarely with her clear blue eyes.

"Your father left us, Robin, because he was a cast-iron first-rate piece of shit; a total abomination made flesh. A very bad choice on my part. You might well have a half-brother – in fact I think you possibly do – but it certainly isn't Jason. You might well have half-sisters too – I wouldn't bet against it. If you must know, your father left us because he already had another family somewhere up North; one he had set up before he even set eyes on me. *We* were the 'other family' – not the other way round. *We* were his dirty secret – not his first family. And who knows how many other families he's had on the go as he drove his truck up and down this green and pleasant land? Your father was an adventurer – and that's putting it kindly. He was a rutting pig – spreading his seed freely wherever he went, treating life as a game and the world as his playground. *That's* the secret I've kept from you – *and* from Jason – all these years after your father left us. *That's* what I've sat on and had to digest after I confronted your 'wonderful' Dad and found out the truth…that my marriage was *bigamous*; that our family life was a sham; that betrayal was a kind of amusing hobby for him. *That's* the secret, Robin – not your paternity. You and Jason *are* full brothers alright. Trust me, as your mother; I should know!"

Now it was my turn to adopt a stunned and silent pose, my mouth hanging loose and open like a newly dead fish.

Chapter 29

Christmas Day 1977 dawned – a day unlike any other. Normally on Christmas Day I would be up with the lark, my stomach turning somersaults in anticipation of presents, roast turkey with all the trimmings, a war movie on the TV and…even more presents.

I would tip-toe downstairs; there would be tinsel, decorations, cards on string stretched out like bunting, carols on the radio. This morning? None of that. Not even close.

Mum woke me at 6.45 a.m sharp with an abrupt knock on the bedroom door. Her head poked round the gap and into the bedroom.

"Robin, are you coming?" she asked in a tone that was less of a question and more of an instruction.

"Wha…?" I mumbled, half awake.

"The hospital. Jason. Come on. Get yourself ready."

I sat up and rubbed my eyes like a cartoon character.

"If you're coming, Robin, get a move on. Breakfast in the kitchen in ten minutes."

The bedroom door closed and she was gone. I almost had to pinch myself to be sure she'd really been there and I wasn't dreaming.

"Merry Christmas, Mum," I muttered to myself, as I was already listening to her footsteps racing frantically down the stairs.

I threw on the first clothes that came to hand – a bright green replica goalkeeper's jersey, black jeans and my *Vans* trainers. I went into the bathroom to spike my hair, brush my teeth and to attempt to convince myself, while staring in the mirror, that I didn't care Jason had ruined Christmas. I didn't entirely succeed. Grumpily, I wandered down to the kitchen, barely within Mum's clearly stipulated 'ten minutes'. I could smell the bacon sarnie on the grill even before I walked in.

"Happy Christmas, darling," Mum said as I entered. She rushed over to hug me. Then, standing back, Mum said: "What on earth are you wearing?"

"My goalie sweater," I said flatly.

"Oh," said Mum, suppressing a chuckle. "I thought you were dressing up as a Christmas tree for Christmas Day!"

"I can change it, if you want," I said.

"No, no, you're alright, love. Wear whatever you want to – it's Christmas Day after all. It's just…well, it's a bit colourful, that's all."

I sat at the kitchen table.

"Merry Christmas Mum," I said. It came out heartfelt, mawkish and flip all at once. Somehow the bizarre tone suited the circumstances but Mum didn't seem to notice. She just ploughed on regardless; pottering about with utensils, looking absent-mindedly in cupboards.

"Bacon sarnie alright for breakfast, Robin?"

"Very Christmassy," I said.

It was meant to be a joke but it came out slightly tinged with spite. Mum threw the knife she was holding into the sink so it made a tremendous clatter.

"Robin, I'm doing my best here. This wasn't the Christmas any of us wanted."

She was holding on to the edge of the sink, as if it was the only thing keeping her upright.

"I'm sorry, Mum," I said. "It was meant to be a joke. It just came out wrong. A bacon sarnie is fine, thanks."

"No, I'm sorry, Robin. I'm *truly* sorry."

She came and sat opposite me at the table and took my hands in hers. She looked me in the eyes.

"Merry Christmas, Robin, love. Let's make it the very best we can."

She shook my hands up and down, like we were two kids playing 'ring-a-roses'. I smiled as indulgently as I could.

"A bacon sarnie would be very nice, thanks."

Mum returned to the cooker and pretty soon I had a glass of orange juice and a round of bacon sarnies set before me. She didn't do Jason's thing of adding *Sarson's* to the sarnie. ("Disgusting," she'd said when she first saw him doing it). Instead, I was presented with a choice of ketchup or brown sauce. I was actually sorely tempted to get up and add some *Sarson's* – I really did like it – but I didn't dare. I smothered the sarnies liberally with brown sauce instead. All Mum had was a cup of tea and a cigarette. She was so thin it was like she was made of twigs. I tried to offer her one of my sarnies. She shook her head and smiled.

"You eat. I made them for you."

As I munched, Mum talked.

"I got you up early as I want you to be ready. Brenda is coming round at 10 a.m. She's giving us a lift to the hospital so we can visit Jason. She'll drop us off then fetch us an hour later – so we'll have to be quick and punctual. It's very good of her to do this, Robin. She's got her own family's Christmas dinner to prepare. She doesn't need to be driving us hither and thither all day like a taxi service – yet she's fully prepared to help out friends in need. That's what friends do, Robin – help each other out. And families should do that too. That's the right thing to do. You and Jason might scoff at my friends from the bridge club but they're good people."

"The only thing I'm scoffing are these sarnies," I replied, spitting crumbs in my eagerness to crack my joke.

"Very funny," Mum said but, despite herself, she chuckled.

I took a big swig of orange juice and looked at my watch.

"We've got ages before 10am," I said in a tone of considerable puzzlement. Mum smiled broadly.

"That's because – once you finish your sandwiches – I want you to come outside to the garage with me. There's something I need you to help me with."

My face must have fallen because Mum's smile quickly changed to an expression of puzzlement at my seeming reluctance. Frankly, after my late night *Guzzi*-nobbling excursion, the garage was the last place I wanted to go – in fact, I'd not even set foot back in there since. However, I could hardly tell Mum that. I took another bite from one of my sandwiches and smiled.

"Sure thing," I mumbled.

"Okay," Mum said. "Well then, I'll see you out there."

She stood up and fetched the garage key from its hook. Then she walked out of the kitchen and disappeared down the side alley. I watched her pass the window as I finished my final sarnie. I felt a bit sick in my stomach but it was nothing to do with the food. I half knew what she wanted me to follow her into the garage for – but I couldn't be certain. A nagging doubt still remained it might have something to do with my attempt to sabotage the *Guzzi*. Surely it couldn't be that – why would it be *that*? Even so, I got up from the kitchen table like a man going before the judge.

Mum was standing at the rear of the garage with the door wide open. She was standing next to a large object covered with a sheet. I walked in slowly, the walk of the condemned, the scenario feeling oddly like something from a horror movie. As I got a few feet from her, Mum suddenly whipped the bed sheet off the object with a flourish. There, revealed in all its glory, was a brand new top-of-the-range tropical fish tank. It must have cost her over a hundred pounds. It was far more than I'd been expecting, much more than I deserved. When I saw it, I burst into tears. To Mum, they were tears of joy. To me, they were tears of relief.

Chapter 30

Brenda Collins was one of Mum's friends from bridge club. They gathered every first Thursday of each month and took it in turns to act as host. I hadn't met many of them but I'd met Brenda before.

I'd actually been in primary school with Brenda's son, Mark. However, once we went to 'big school' (as Brenda insisted on calling it) we'd lost touch as Mark and I went to different places.

Mark and I had never been great friends but, because our Mums socialised and we went to the same school, we used to play at each other's houses after school sometimes. Mostly we played *Subbuteo* or 'soldiers'. 'Soldiers' was our own invention. We'd line up all these *Airfix* soldiers from World War Two – German Paratroopers v British Commandos – and then we'd throw dice (we had one die each, taken out of one of Mark's board games). Whatever the score on the die was, that was the exact number of soldiers you could 'kill' by knocking them over. If you threw a three, you could knock over three soldiers.

Then it was the other person's turn. If they threw a four, they could knock over four of your soldiers. If you threw a six, you had a choice. You could either choose to drop a battery (Mark took it out of his parents' radio in their bedroom) from shoulder height directly onto the lines of enemy soldiers (to simulate an air attack) or you could elect to throw the die again. If you threw again and got a six, you could 'capture' the enemy 'General' (one soldier was nominated as the General before the game began and set back 'behind the lines'). If you captured the 'General' then, every time you threw your die, you got to kill two extra soldiers (so, if you threw a three, you could kill five soldiers, and, if you threw a six, you could kill eight soldiers).

If your General was captured and you threw a six, you could throw again. If you got another six then your 'raiding party' was deemed to have released your General. It all got quite complicated but it was definitely my favourite game whenever I went round to Mark's house.

Mark got sent to a boarding school – not a big name one; a small one that specialised in sports. I couldn't imagine that – being sent away from home for months on end but Mark adapted quite quickly, according to his Mum. Mark's dad had been at the same school and he was keen for his son to follow in his footsteps. That was mainly why Mark and I lost contact but, the couple of times I'd seen Mark since then, I'd figured we wouldn't get on. Mark had grown his hair really long and liked 'prog rock' – *Genesis* and *Yes*. He'd also started talking with a sort of posh accent – not massively but a bit. Jason had seen him once and said: "Who's that poof? He's an even bigger poof than you, LB!" It was hard not to disagree. I know it was shallow but the 'prog rock' put me off more than the long hair. Now we'd outgrown 'soldiers' what on earth would we talk about?

Brenda drove an *Austin 1100* estate car. She drove in a neurotic fashion, with her nose pressed against the windscreen as if she couldn't see properly (even though there was nothing wrong with her eyes). When she gave me a lift home after I'd been round their house playing 'soldiers' with Mark, Mark would refuse to go in the car, screaming: "I'm too young to die!" Sometimes Brenda had to give me a lift home without Mark. When Brenda turned up to give me and Mum a lift to the hospital, she was driving the very same car.

I sat in the back, listening to the two women talk. After wishing each other a 'Merry Christmas' and after Mum asked politely how Mark was doing at school (top of this and top of that apparently), their chat was focused mainly on Jason and the accident. After a while, I screened them out as far as I could and just stared dumbly out of the window at households enjoying their Christmas while remaining totally oblivious to my family's drama. I still couldn't believe it was actually Christmas Day.

Presently we arrived at the hospital. Brenda let us out in the car park.

"I'll be back in an hour," she called to Mum, leaning across from the driver's seat to pull the passenger door shut. "Are you sure that's long enough?"

"Plenty thanks, Brenda, really," Mum replied. "You've got your own family to think of. It's Christmas Day, we've put you to enough trouble. Thank you so much once again."

Unseen by Brenda, Mum dug me in the ribs. I took the hint.

"Thank you Auntie Brenda," I said, leaning into the car and smiling.

She wasn't my aunt but I'd been encouraged to call her that when I was a kid and it had stuck as a kind of 'in-joke'. Brenda smiled.

"See you in an hour. Give Jason my best." Then she was gone.

"Is it really worth her going away for just an hour? What can she do in that time?" I asked Mum.

"She's going to put the turkey in the oven then she's coming straight back for us. She's giving up part of her Christmas to help us out, Robin. It's very Christian of her. You can't easily get a minicab on Christmas Day and I didn't know who else to ask. Brenda didn't hesitate."

"Can't Mr. Collins put the turkey in the oven?" I asked.

"Ha!" my mother laughed. It seemed to be the funniest joke she'd heard all year. Mum grabbed my hand and we walked into the hospital together.

I'm convinced there's nothing on earth quite so depressing as a hospital on Christmas Day. All the decorations looked worn and faded – as though they were all fifteen years old rather than brand new – and all the visitors wore pained expressions of forced jollity and horrific rictus grins at complete odds with the pain, discomfort and distress of the loved ones they were visiting. I felt like shutting my eyes as we made our way up to Jason and Cherry's floor.

Before Brenda had arrived to give us a lift and after I'd been given my brand new fish tank, I'd sat with Mum again in the kitchen.

"Are we taking Jason a Christmas present?" I'd asked Mum. She'd laughed dismissively.

"After what he said to you, he'll be lucky I don't throw him out the window! No, his present is our visit – seeing his loving family on Christmas Day. We'll see just what he deserves once he comes home. He's got a lot of bridges to build, Robin, one heck of a lot of damage to repair."

I'd nodded quietly and extracted a promise from Mum that I could be the first one to go in and see Jason – and that I could do so on my own. I'd added that meantime perhaps Mum could go and see Cherry – see if she was alright and wish her a 'Happy Christmas' from me. I was surprised Mum had agreed without question. I'd expected a big argument about it but I guess Mum realised I had things to say to Jason that I just didn't want to say in front of her. Either way, once we got to Jason's room, I went in alone.

Chapter 31

"Merry fucking Christmas!" said Jason when he saw me walking into his room. "Have you come dressed as a Christmas tree, you little prick?"

"Mum's done that joke already," I said nonchalantly, sitting on the chair beside his bed.

He still looked bruised – and unusually weedy – more vulnerable than I'd ever seen him. Even so, he retained a wiry strength and I didn't doubt he remained a physical danger to me. However, I was suffused with a strange kind of confidence that went beyond bravado via rage to a deadly calm. I *wanted* to confront him – I'd come here actively *seeking* it.

"Where's Mum?" Jason asked.

"Seeing Cherry," I said casually. I felt like putting my feet on his bed, but didn't quite dare.

"Probably putting down the poison, spinning a pack of lies about me," Jason sneered.

"You really are a bit of crap, aren't you?" I said, edging my chair back just a little for safety's sake. Jason couldn't believe I'd actually said that. His mouth gaped.

"What did you just say to me?" he snarled.

He tried to reach out and grab me but it clearly caused him some pain. He caught his breath sharply and fell back against the pillows.

"You heard. I said you're a piece of crap. You always have been and you probably always will be. You never have a nice word to say about anyone, do you?"

Jason surveyed me through narrow eyes. He seemed to be trying to make sense of a world turned upside down all of a sudden.

"Fuck off," he growled eventually. "If you've only come here to hurl abuse at me on Christmas Day, LB, you can fuck right off. Go on, get lost. I didn't ask you to come here, you little wanker."

"That's rich," I replied, standing up but still maintaining a careful distance. "I never asked for any of the shit you've been heaping on me for years – *years* – but I've had to just take it. Well, now it's your turn."

Annoyingly, my voice wavered. I'd hoped to keep my cool. Jason laughed.

"Oh, boo hoo! My heart bleeds! Man up, you little turd. You're very brave, all of a sudden, aren't you? Now I'm in a hospital bed, you've finally found the balls to stick up for yourself. Very impressive, I don't think."

I walked to the window and stared out, keeping my back to him. Outside an ambulance was unloading an old man on a stretcher and wheeling him into the hospital. I saw it happening but the scene didn't really register – it was just a kind of blurry motion far below. I was too focused on what Jason might say next and how this whole scene was going to play out between us.

"You wait until I get out, LB. You're in for the biggest fucking hiding I've ever given you. I'm gonna…"

I spun round and approached him, my fist raised like a hammer.

"You'll do *what*? What'cha gonna *do*, big man?" I yelled.

To my surprise, Jason flinched and shrank back. It astonished me so much that I'd successfully provoked this reaction from him that I lost my ire almost immediately. I sat back down in the chair next to him.

"You know, *when* you get out of here – which could be weeks from what I've heard – you'll more than likely be stuck in a wheelchair," I said in the most convincing 'by-the-way' tone I could manage. "In fact, you *might* never leave that wheelchair. Then you'll be the one at *my* mercy – day in day out, week in week out. *You* dependent on *me*. Imagine that. Imagine the *revenge* I could get if I was even remotely like you."

I leaned back in the chair, sated and spent. I was practically breathless.

Jason seemed to be giving my words some serious consideration. He was silent – and cowed – for quite some time.

"Just go," he said eventually.

"I'm sorry?" I asked, cupping my hand to my ear with cod theatricality.

"Just go, will you?" Jason said in an unusually small voice.

I clasped my hands behind my head and stretched my legs, making it abundantly clear I was going nowhere anytime soon. In some ways, I actually appalled myself – I was now terrorising Jason in the exact same way he had terrorised me. I was supposed to be better than that.

I had to take control; I had to be myself again. This wasn't who I was. I put my head in my hands and rocked forward with my head practically on my knees. If Jason was watching me, he was doing so in total silence. I seemed to be motionless like that for a very long time. Eventually, I surfaced. I rubbed my face as though I'd just been washing in a sink. I looked Jason squarely in the eyes.

"It's not true, you know." I said firmly but calmly.

"What?" Jason asked. It was still a small voice, not combative.

"It's not true. I asked Mum. You probably thought I wouldn't. You probably banked on it, didn't you?"

Jason swallowed and looked panicked – if he could have run away, he would have done so. I continued: "We *are* brothers."

I held Jason's gaze – eyeball to eyeball. I was waiting for the usual comeback; the one-liner, the snide remark, the spiteful jibe, the barbed insult. However, Jason remained silent. Instead – and to my utter astonishment – he suddenly began to *cry*.

It was a whiney, high-pitched kind of crying – oddly girly and childish – uncomfortable to behold in a previously swaggering youth. He put a hand up to his face and gripped his nose in an effort to stem the flow of tears. It looked like he was trying to stifle a nosebleed. I was transfixed by this unexpected development. My stomach lurched.

Somehow this was worse than any of our verbal combat.

Immediately I regretted all I'd said and done to cause this. I wanted to go to him and comfort him but I sat immobile and paralysed – still a little bit afraid.

"I'm so sorry, Robin." Jason sniffed. "I'm sorry. I don't know what else to say."

I shifted in my seat and looked at the door, hoping some deity might enter and magically roll back time – make this whole scene go away; fix things so this confrontation had never happened. I thought about leaving but my legs suddenly seemed just as useless as Jason's.

"It's going to be different. I promise you, LB." Jason was burbling. "When I come out I'm going to put it right. All the wrong I've done, I'm going to put it all right."

I waved a hand at him dismissively – not to denigrate his words but to show he didn't need to say anything more on the subject. I'd kicked a man while he was down quite enough – I didn't need to see him crawl. I bit deeply into one of my own knuckles, hoping he would stop. Suddenly, seemingly spontaneously, Jason held both arms open.

"Come here *brother*. Let's start over."

The offer: seemingly magnanimous; a noble gesture; a sight I thought I'd never see emanating from Jason unbidden. More than a truce; an offer of a clean slate. But could I really trust it? Was this just another trick – like so many of the tricks and stunts Jason had pulled on me so many times before?

Could I really allow myself to fall for the whole 'olive branch' routine yet again? Was this just another Trojan Horse? Could I take the risk of rising from this chair, climbing onto the bed, embracing him and then…getting my ear bitten off, my eyes gouged or whatever assault Jason deemed fitting for the 'humiliation' I'd just visited upon him? Should I *really* take that risk? Jason stretched his arms wider, his eyes imploring me.

I stood up. A showdown began – both within myself and between us as brothers. This was no easy decision. I walked slowly to the bed. I sat down slowly on the edge of the bed, being extra careful not to put any weight on Jason's damaged limbs. I thought of something Mum used to say: "Think as our Lord would think, act as our Lord would act. If repentance is genuine, you have a duty to forgive." The problem was, telling if the 'repentance' was actually genuine or not.

I sank, trembling, into Jason's arms, closing my eyes, waiting for the violence he was sure to unleash. Was this repentance genuine? Somehow I doubted it. Jason's arms closed around me – vice-like in strength despite his injuries. His mouth moved ever closer to my ear until I could feel his breath, his teeth bared.

"Merry fucking Christmas, Robin…you *little bastard*!"

It was said with affection, not venom. And so we both laughed – and we laughed and we laughed and we *laughed*…until that hospital bed shook on its rusty hinges.

Chapter 32

Once we were home, to my surprise, Mum told me everything she'd said to Cherry whereas I told her almost nothing about what I'd said to Jason. To my further surprise, Mum didn't attempt to pry any further. She simply accepted at face value that Jason and I had called a truce and were now on a new and better footing, no doubt praying silently (as I did too) that it would last.

"We're okay now, me and Jason." I'd told her in a voice close to rapture when she'd walked in on us laughing our heads off and hugging on his hospital bed. Jason had even ruffled my hair in a paternal fashion, as if to provide visual evidence of the truth of my statement.

"There's no better gift I could have for Christmas," Mum said, smiling benignly at "my boys" as she proudly called us. Then she added: "Go and wait outside now, Robin. I need to speak to your brother alone for a bit."

"Can I go and see Cherry?" I asked, bouncing off the bed in my eagerness to give Cherry the news that Jason and I had finally discovered our fraternal feelings.

"No," said Mum, firmly. "Cherry's resting and she's not to be disturbed right now. I told her 'Merry Christmas' from you. You just wait outside, Robin, there's a good lad. Brenda will be here soon and we need to leave the moment she arrives – it won't do to keep her waiting when she's doing us a big favour on Christmas Day. Five minutes, Robin, that's all I need. Now, run along."

"Merry Christmas," I said to Jason as I left.

"Merry Christmas, LB." Jason replied, with a quick wave.

For years I could never have imagined such a scene unfolding between us. Maybe Christmas really was the time of miracles, after all.

I sat outside Jason's room on a plastic chair by the door. The door had his name on it – a small piece of card bearing the legend 'Jason Bellamy' in black marker pen slotted into a gilt frame. I now looked upon his name fondly – almost with new eyes. It somehow helped that it was surrounded by holly and tinsel. I stared at it for perhaps a full five minutes until Mum emerged. She smoothed her coat and fished in her handbag for her cigarettes.

"Come on, Robin," she said. "Look lively. Brenda could be outside right now and I'm gasping for a quick fag before she gets here."

Mum was lucky on that score – Brenda didn't appear for another ten minutes and, as we stood in the car park, Mum had two cigarettes in quick succession. She smoked nervously, her hand shaking slightly and her puffing short, sharp and insistent. I tried to ask her about Cherry but it was not until we got home that we spoke on that topic. Instead, Mum worked to steer the conversation elsewhere.

"I got you another Christmas present, you know." Mum said. "Besides the fish tank, that is – a secret one."

Now she had my attention! My curiosity was awoken and I was successfully distracted. From an inauspicious start, this was turning into perhaps my best Christmas ever.

"What is it?" I wheedled, like a child.

"Ah!" Mum smiled enigmatically. "You'll have to wait and see, won't you. Otherwise it wouldn't be a secret, would it?"

I watched Mum smoke, imagining all sorts of gifts – some unlikely (a bicycle, a top of the range skateboard), others more prosaic but no less well received (a cartridge pen for school, a pair of football socks). I was still imagining – an array of possible and unlikely gifts swirling through my mind like the conveyor belt on *The Generation Game* – when Brenda turned up in her *Austin 1100*, carving a wide semi-circle across the car park before pulling up in front of us like a cabbie at an airport terminal.

I screened out the women's chatter on the journey back – I was way too much in thrall to the unexpected developments of my truce with Jason and the mystery Christmas present awaiting me at home to bother trying to eavesdrop on the women's nonsensical twittering. Even the scenery passed in a blur, such was the 'high' I felt at that moment. Finally, it seemed, everything really was going to be alright in the Bellamy household at long, long last.

Once Brenda's car pulled up at our house, I lost count of the number of times she asked Mum and me to go over to her house for Christmas dinner.

"No, no, thank you Brenda," Mum pleaded. "I've imposed on you and your family quite enough for one Christmas. I really appreciate the offer but I'm going to cook Robin his Christmas meal – we don't want that going to waste – and I need to stay by the phone in case there's any news from the hospital. But, thank you, really."

Mum took hold of Brenda's hands in both of hers and squeezed gently.

"We're both very grateful, aren't we, Robin?" Mum called to me, waking me from my gift-imaginings.

"Yes, yes. Thank you Mrs Collins…er…Auntie Brenda." I answered. "Merry Christmas." I added – a high-pitched afterthought.

The two women laughed indulgently at my Pavlovian response. We waved enthusiastically as Mrs Collins disappeared towards the end of our road, crunching her car's gears as she went.

"Such a lovely woman," Mum sighed. "A true friend."

Mum put an arm around my shoulders and led me to the front door. Once inside, Mum said: "Come and help me in the kitchen, Robin. While I fix the food, I'll tell you what Cherry and I had to say to each other."

That was an offer I simply couldn't refuse and I practically tripped over my own feet in my rush to the kitchen; my extra Christmas present temporarily forgotten.

Chapter 33

If I'm honest, I wasn't much help to Mum in the kitchen. I was put to work peeling things – potatoes, parsnips, carrots and such. The problem was, I was both slow and messy.

So, as usual, Mum ended up doing most of the work herself while I just watched. I don't think she minded too much, though. She seemed happy enough just to have my company and I certainly felt the same about her. As Mum bustled about, I sat at the kitchen table totally riveted as she told me about her conversation with Cherry in the hospital. I felt thrilled Mum was freely including me in what she'd normally have deemed to be purely 'adult talk'.

"If I tell you this, Robin, you have to solemnly promise not to repeat it to anyone – including Jason."

Such was my eagerness to know more about Cherry, I couldn't promise quickly enough. My pledge proffered, Mum began.

"I told Cherry straight: 'He's not good enough for you, Cherry. I know he's my son but he's trouble. He's not right in the head – don't ask me how I know. I'm here to warn you off once and for all.' That's what I told her."

I nearly fell off my chair. I hadn't expected that. I was also filled with a terror that, if Cherry listened to Mum, I might never see her again.

"What did she say to that?" I blurted. Mum laughed; a happy laugh, not in the least scornful.

"She said: 'Blimey Mrs B, that's one heck of a greeting. No 'how are you'? No 'Merry Christmas'? And where are my grapes or at least a slice of Christmas cake?' She's a bright one, that girl. Well, I had to laugh. Way too good for Jason, she is. Way, *way* too good for your brother, I'm afraid."

I couldn't disagree – although, with my new-found détente with Jason, I now found myself very slightly aggrieved on his behalf.

"Then what?" I asked.

This was like a proper soap opera – a real-life drama that meant something and impacted on real lives – not like all that *Crossroads* and *Coronation Street* rubbish Mum watched on telly.

"Well, then I apologised to the girl," Mum continued. "That was no way for me to greet her on Christmas Day. I really should have been more thoughtful. So I asked her how she was feeling."

"And?" I asked, literally on the edge of my seat.

"Robin, don't interrupt me all the time, there's a good lad – else I'll never finish."

To distract myself, I picked up the salt cellar and began turning it around in my fingers like a set of worry beads.

"Okay," said Mum, satisfied I was now finally just a passive listener. "So, I asked Cherry how she was and she said: 'I'll live – as will Jason, I hope.' And then she fixed me with a steady gaze and added: 'Listen, Mrs B, with all due respect, I know your son, Jason, inside out. I'm under no illusions. I'm in this relationship with my eyes open – both of them. He's not like he is with others when he's with me, I promise you. Trust me, I wouldn't stick around if he was. I know he's not perfect but he needs me and I'm good for him too. I probably shouldn't say this to you but rumour has it – well, my dad says anyway – that you married quite a rum 'un yourself.' Well…"

I started to interrupt again but Mum raised a hand to stop me.

"Well," Mum continued. "I couldn't really argue with her on that. So I said: all the more reason we need a woman-to-woman talk, my girl. I know exactly what I'm saving you from. Well, then she said: 'I don't need saving, Mrs B. You really don't think people can change for the better, do you?' I replied that she could learn from my experience and that, while change was not impossible it was extremely rare. I said it was the naivety and idealism of youth to expect to triumph against the odds – to believe that a leopard can change its spots. And she said: 'It's love, Mrs B. Don't expect it to be rational or sensible or reasonable because I don't.' Well, you could have knocked me down with a feather. Love, she said! She's in *love* with him. There's no arguing there, then. Nothing I could say would remove her from his side if it's *love* we're talking about – even though he'd almost killed her on that damned motorbike he loves so much."

A cold chill ran through me at the mention of the *Guzzi*. All the residual guilt I thought I'd conquered suddenly came rushing back in a flood. I felt sick and dizzy. I put the salt cellar back on the table and pinched myself on the thigh to regain my composure. Mum hadn't noticed my momentary distress and carried on speaking as she ran the turkey under the cold tap before adding seasoning.

"So, there was nothing more to be said, was there?"

I recognised this was a purely rhetorical question and allowed Mum to continue.

"So I simply told her: 'Well, you know where I am and you can always rely on me. I'm on *your* side, you know. He's my boy but he needs to grow up and start treating other people properly and he needs to start doing it pretty damn soon. And please, lovey, call me Rose. And get well soon, love, won't you.' And then I turned to leave. And then, at the door, I had a sudden thought and so I turned back to her and I said: 'Cherry, love, you're not?...' Cherry laughed. 'No. Good God, no. No, I certainly hope not!' Then she paused and said to me ever so sadly: 'There was some doubt, you know, after the accident, if I could ever....well...they tell me it should be okay. Probably, it should.' So I nodded. I said: 'I'd like a grandchild one day. Not yet though!' And then I said to her: 'Robin's enough of a handful right now!'

At this point Mum walked over and put her arms around me, as if to reassure me in case I'd been offended by that last remark. But I hadn't been offended; it had clearly been a joke and I'd recognised it as such. And besides, that wasn't Mum's intention anyway. Instead she said to me, while hugging me close:

"Do you know what Cherry said to me in reply?"

I shook my head.

"She said: 'Robin's a star, Rose. You should be very proud of him.' So, there you are – don't let it swell your head though, will you?"

Then Mum released me, smiled and returned to preparing the turkey for the oven.

I was ecstatic. Cherry had actually said that? She'd said I'm a 'star'? Coming from her, it was all the confirmation I needed. A *star*! This was definitely the best Christmas ever…and then it suddenly got even better.

Mum said: "Now, how about I find you that extra Christmas present I got you? Just let me put this bird in the oven then I'll fetch it."

Chapter 34

My secret present was one of the best ever – every bit as good as the new fish tank. I decided it was a dead heat between them – because nothing could ever really eclipse the fish tank (which was beyond brilliant). My secret present was a *Polaroid* camera. It was the height of technology – the zenith of what was possible with film. Instant pictures – imagine that! It was a magic box – filled with arcane chemical compounds woven into special paper, sprinkled with stardust. I was ecstatic.

Mum presented it to me and watched me unwrap it while the turkey cooked and luscious fumes of crispy skin, crunchy roast potatoes and bubbling gravy juices permeated the entire house. The camera was wrapped in silver paper featuring multiple images of Santa in his sleigh interspersed with jolly snowmen. That wrapping paper lasted about a nanosecond before it became a shredded pile of litter on the floor and I proudly held my new camera aloft.

It came in a square cardboard box emblazoned with a picture of the camera bordered by a diagonal rainbow-coloured stripe. The camera inside was wrapped in polythene and smelled oddly of a new car interior. There was an instruction manual in three different languages – English, German and French – which I pored over as though it were a newly discovered religious text.

Mum was overjoyed at my own joy and I hugged and kissed her as though I were five years old again.

"Thank you, thank you and thank you once again," I said. "It's brilliant. I'd never have guessed what it was – not in a zillion trillion years."

"I'm just happy to see you happy, Robin." Mum beamed. "This has been a very difficult time for all of us. Now we need to move forward – together. We need to create some new, happy memories and you can record them for us on your brand new camera."

"Will do!" I assured her.

I could hardly put the camera down long enough to eat my Christmas meal. I used it to take a picture of the dinner Mum had cooked and another of the two Christmas crackers we shared and a close-up shot of a smiling Mum wearing her paper hat, obligatory fag in hand. Then I taught Mum how to use the camera so she could take a picture of me, kneeling beside my new fish tank, my smile wider than the Sargasso Sea (wherever that was!).

Mum had asked Brenda to pop out and buy the camera for her on Christmas Eve – talk about an inspired last minute purchase. She'd collected it from Brenda while we were getting a lift to and from the hospital. I hadn't spotted the handover between them – their sleight of hand was as skilful as a pair of stage magicians – nor I had I twigged Mum was carrying a larger handbag than usual for the hospital visit.

The camera was brilliant – there was no other word that could do it justice. It was so brilliant I figured I'd grow up to become a photographer; maybe even one who specialises in photographing tropical fish.

By the time I went to bed that night, I had pictures I'd taken of my mother and my Christmas feast pinned on the back of my bedroom door. No long wait for the chemist to send my film away to the developers – only to discover half of the images came back blurry, over-exposed and covered in stickers labelling them as 'rejects'. This was a new age of photography: instant, magical, brilliant – this was the *future*! It also gave me an idea.

A few days later, on December 30th, before another new year was upon us, I took, with Mum's permission, a bus to the hospital to see Jason and Cherry on my own while Mum opened the salon for a few of her regulars who wanted to fix up their hair for New Year's Eve. I'd set aside some of the special paper for my *Polaroid* camera and I packed the paper and camera very carefully into my *Adidas* bag, protecting it from any bumps by wrapping it in an old sweatshirt.

When I arrived at the hospital, I went straight to Cherry's room. I know I should have visited Jason first but the lure of Cherry was just too strong. She was so pleased to see me and, knowing she'd called me a 'star', I was further emboldened when I saw her and, for once, felt able to talk to her straight out and with none of the embarrassment I'd felt from earlier when I'd imagined that she knew I also imagined her as 'Sally from Penge'.

Now, I just talked to Cherry like an actual person – like one person to another; *normal*. I told her I was pleased she was staying with Jason and that I hoped she'd get well soon and "come home" (which meant our house). I showed her the *Polaroid* camera, removing it from my bag like a rare Egyptian artefact, discovered in the pyramids and smuggled to England at great peril.

My only note of disappointment was that Cherry refused my request to snap her picture her with it. (I'd been dreaming of her acquiescence in that regard ever since I'd received the camera). She did manage to sugar-coat her refusal and let me down gently, though.

"Not like this, Robin," she'd laughed. "All trussed up and bandaged in hospital, bruised and without any make-up? No way! You're not going to blackmail me with those images. When I come out, I'll happily pose for as many pictures as you like but not topless ones, mind!"

Despite myself, I blushed at her reference to her going topless. I hugged her quickly and rushed off to see Jason. This was going to be the real litmus test. Could I *really* trust Jason with my new camera?

If I handed it to him, would he 'accidentally' drop it on the floor or just smash it up in front of me? Had the leopard really changed its spots or was his previous display of 'brotherly affection' all an act to get back in Mum's good books after all the awful stuff he'd said about Dad and my parentage?

I guess there was only one way to find out.

I had butterflies in my guts as I pushed open the door to Jason's hospital bedroom.

"Well, well, well," he said as I entered. "Look what the cat dragged in."

It was neutral in tone – inscrutable – but a hint of a smile gave me confidence as I approached his bedside. We chatted for a while about Mum and Christmas – largely talking all around each other. I think it was awkward for him too – being nice to me (or even pretending to be) was something he'd not done for years. This was alien to us both. I told Jason how great Mum's Christmas meal had been but then quickly realised I'd made a tactical error.

"Hospital food's shite," he deadpanned. "My Christmas dinner was some bit of old shoe leather floating in *Bisto*. May as well have had a fucking *Pot Noodle!*"

And then we both laughed. We laughed like drains; we laughed like we'd laughed when we'd hugged each other on Christmas Day.

Perhaps, I thought, this was the time to take the risk of showing him my new camera. I took it from my bag, then pulled it from its box and placed it on the palm of my hand. I held it out to Jason.

"Look what Mum got me for Christmas," I said.

Jason took it from me and twirled it around in his fingers, examining it this way and that. Internally, I winced. My insides rose up into my throat. It took all the strength I possessed not to snatch the camera straight back from Jason and return it instantly to the relative sanctuary of my *Adidas* bag.

I'd tried to prepare myself psychologically for coping if Jason smashed the camera out of spite. If that happened, I'd go back to Mum and tell her what Jason had done and he'd be finished with her then (at least I had that much insurance, I figured).

However, now that he held my latest pride and joy in his hands, I realised there was no psychological preparation for something so traumatic happening right before your eyes. I just had to grit my teeth and live through the moment. Eventually, after what seemed an eternity, Jason handed the camera back to me unharmed.

"Pretty cool," he stated. Then: "Come on, then. What are you waiting for? Take my picture!"

There was none of Cherry's reticence. Immediately he was striking poses – he always had been a poseur (even he'd admit that) –

and as fast as I could take one shot he'd adopt a new position as though fashion modelling was in his blood. I had to admit, even in hospital garb, he looked good and took a mean picture; would that I had been even half as photogenic.

He loved watching the pictures develop – the harsh white frame and central black panel eventually yielding to a preening Jason; charismatic and handsome even while bruised and bandaged.

Before I left, I told him Cherry had said that she loved him. He looked at me and winked.

"Everyone does, kiddo," he grinned. "Everyone does. Now, close the door on your way out!"

I was summarily dismissed but that was okay because I'd be leaving happy and on a high – not booted coldly into the corridor at home to crawl back to my own bedroom. Those days, I hoped, were gone.

On the way home, I changed buses twice and took a purposeful detour – I was a man on a mission. I got on the number 33 and headed out to Barnes. I knew exactly where I was going – to the scene of Jason and Cherry's accident. I was headed for the Bolan tree. Jason and Cherry had crashed on the exact same stretch of road that had claimed Marc's life. What were the odds? It kind of freaked me out.

I got off the bus in Upper Richmond Road and walked up the lane to the little humped bridge where the tree stood. Jason and Cherry had come off the *Guzzi* a bit beyond the tree and I'd just walked past the exact spot where they'd almost died.

It was the tree I wanted, though. It stood there like a sentinel; a silent witness to a moment of horror and tragedy and loss. It had already been turned into a shrine. There were rosettes and ribbons and pictures of Marc Bolan pinned to tree trunk.

The base of the tree was surrounded by toys – stuffed plush green frogs, a few swans, other soft toys, lots of teddies and a few plastic wizards. There were handwritten notes – proclamations of undying love and promises never to forget.

I'd loved Bolan too – or, at least, his music – but my mission today was different. I pulled a drawing pin from one of the notes that had been left for Marc, carefully re-pinning the note beneath another one (I would never have dreamed of jettisoning it). Then, I extracted one of my *Polaroid* shots of Jason in the hospital from my *Adidas* bag – an image of Jason grinning madly while clasping both arms behind his head. I pinned Jason's picture to the Bolan tree, making sure it was stuck fast. Then, I took out a biro and carefully wrote across the space below: "I love you, Big Brother."

THE END

Author's Note

Little Bastard is my third published novel. It took me approximately eight years to write and first appeared as three chapters of a work-in-progress on the (now defunct) Harper Collins authors' community website, Authonomy. The strong support and consistently positive feedback *Little Bastard* received on Authonomy encouraged me to persevere with the novel, finally completing the fully realised work in December 2015.

Little Bastard spans a six-month period in London in 1977 – from the Queen's Silver Jubilee to Christmas/New Year. It charts the increasing levels of friction between a bullying older brother, Jason, and his long-suffering younger sibling, Robin. The book has its dark moments but I felt it was important to lighten the story with plenty of black humour – reflecting the light and shade we all encounter in our everyday reality.

The idea for *Little Bastard* emerged – as with each of my novels thus far – wholly out of the ether as I neared completion of my previous book, the concept thriller *Love, Gudrun Ensslin*. I remain fascinated by this phenomenon – books emerging as virtually complete concepts as I near the end of any given writing project. Pretentious as it sounds, my experience so far has truly been a case of the core idea for each novel seemingly appearing from nowhere and 'asking to be written'. The upshot of this process is I am unlikely ever to be pigeonholed as a genre writer.

Little Bastard has something in common with my debut novel, *Rude Boy*. *Rude Boy* is a gritty rites-of-passage tale set in the early 1980s, featuring a protagonist who is even more troubled than *Little Bastard's* Robin. The differences are pronounced – unlike *Little Bastard*, *Rude Boy* prominently features drug use and drug culture and is explicit in a way *Little Bastard* is not. Also, I am a more practised novelist now than I was when *Rude Boy* was written; in terms of craft, *Little Bastard* is the far superior book. Nevertheless, some of the similarities between the two books are striking – even for their author. Both are set in London, both feature sensitive and introspective teenage protagonists whose deteriorating outer lives of conflict and disorder contrast with hidden inner lives that, while troubled, nevertheless offer the hope of redemption. It is fair to say that, in my writing career thus far, I appear to be especially interested in exploring and giving voice to the outsider, the outcast; the rebel with a heart of gold.

Little Bastard is multi-layered yet it works equally well on a superficial level as an entertaining (even nostalgic) yarn that opens a window on a bygone era. I shaped it that way; while writing I was conscious of aiming to produce a book that could be all things to all readers (as far as is actually possible); a story that would reward the reader to a degree precisely commensurate with both their expectations and their individual propensity for textual analysis. I wanted the finished novel to have commercial and populist appeal but I also wanted it to have intellectual depth.

In purely allegorical terms, *Little Bastard* may be seen as a study of masculinity and its changing role in a society that has transitioned from the analogue era of the 1970s to the digital age of the 21st century. In this analysis, Jason and Robin represent two sides of the masculine whole – not only is Jason the 'instinctual' side and Robin the 'cerebral' side but also, in effect, Jason is 'the past' and Robin is 'the future'.

I was aware of this 'Jekyll & Hyde' metaphor (and its direct influence on the narrative) while writing *Little Bastard*. Crucially, however, I didn't want to allow my novel (or its two male protagonists) to be reduced simply to one-dimensional polar opposites. Thus, it is Robin who is the more priapic of the brothers – his erotic obsession with Cherry not only resulting from his age and raging hormones but also rooted in a pure and instinctive masculine drive. I felt it necessary– conceptually and for the sake of realism – to give Robin this characteristic; it gave him complexity, which gave him veracity.

The thematic sub-text concerning masculinity does not, I hope, dominate at the expense of my female characters. I am satisfied my female characters are just as well drawn, realistic and memorable as their male counterparts. I am very fond of the foursome I have created to inhabit this particular kitchen sink drama – Robin, Jason, Rose and Cherry. I currently teach Creative Writing in popular self-devised evening classes at Richmond Adult & Community College in

Surrey and frequently remind my students of the importance of creating three-dimensional fully-fleshed characters that speak with a distinctive individual voice. Hopefully I have practised what I preach in this book!

A further dimension to *Little Bastard* lies in its recreation and exploration of the 1970s in Great Britain. I lived through the 70s in London – although I was a child (slightly younger than Robin) I remember it well. It was a unique decade – one that arguably had repercussions that remain in evidence to this day.

One of the most fascinating aspects to the 1970s (looking back) is that it was the final ever pre-computer and pre-internet age for humanity. That fact gave the era a certain brand of innocence – knowledge and information (on a global scale) was simply unavailable to the masses at the mere touch of a button; people lived with a greater need to trust what they were told by the powers-that-be (no matter how misplaced that trust). At the same time, the 1970s was an era of rebellion evincing a generalised desire for greater social freedoms following the consumer-led economic boom of the 1960s.

However, the 1970s was a deeply schizophrenic age (not least in Britain) – with an undoubted dark side. On one hand, the 1970s in the UK was a time of great individuality and creativity (especially in popular music) and an era in which the emancipation of oppressed peoples (who were derided or disadvantaged for reasons of race, colour, gender or sexual orientation) was high on the agenda and the collective subconscious of wider society. On the other hand, the 1970s was also a time of overt racism, industrial strife, extreme poverty (especially in Scotland and the North), political dissent and violent conflict. I feel I have captured this potent mix within the pages of *Little Bastard* – the casual racism (on mainstream television as well as in playgrounds, pubs and the workplace), the rampant smoking, the burgeoning availability (and widespread social acceptance) of pornography, the hair-trigger threat of violence (on the terraces, at pub closing time) and the central importance of popular music (and musical sub-cultures) to youth culture (in a way that will likely never recur in the modern internet age). This is the world Robin and Jason inhabit.

I am always grateful for feedback from readers. I especially enjoy receiving reviews on Amazon and I will be immensely grateful to those of you who can kindly find the time to leave an Amazon review of *Little Bastard* for me.

Before signing off this Author's Note, there are several people I need to thank. The list is far longer than those treasured few named here (...you'll know who you are amigos!) but there are still one or two individuals I do wish to publically acknowledge. They are: the late Hector (for eternal inspiration), Rosa and Leah (for kindly donating the hardware on which this novel was written – and Leah for editing work across several drafts) and my fellow author Poppet. I would also like to thank all those fellow authors on the Authonomy website who took the time to read and comment on the first three chapters of Little Bastard and thereby play an early and instrumental role in helping to shape the completed novel of today. Finally, I'd like to thank each of my students on the 'Exploring Creative Writing' course at RACC – devising, revising and delivering this course has undoubtedly made me a better writer. Thank you to you all.

And finally, as an author I like to donate a percentage of my own profits from each of my novels to a charitable cause that is making a positive difference to our world, often against increasingly tough odds. Accordingly, I will be donating a percentage of my profits from sales of *Little Bastard* to CHAT – the Celia Hammond Animal Trust; a UK-based animal rescue, welfare and protection charity (with a non-destruction policy) for cats and dogs.

Simon Corbin
December 2015

About The Author

Simon Corbin is an author from southwest London. Simon was educated at Rugby School, London University and Cambridge University. Simon spent over 20 years as a freelance writer/journalist (writing feature articles for newspapers and magazines and completing copywriting assignments for advertising agencies, government departments and blue chip clients) before moving into teaching. (Simon currently teaches both journalism and creative writing at Richmond Adult & Community College in Surrey).

Writing novels has always been a key ambition for Simon – finally becoming a practical reality at the age of 25 when Simon began writing his first published novel, *Rude Boy*. This was followed by the concept thriller *Love, Gudrun Ensslin*. Never one to be hidebound by genre, Simon's next novel, *Black Dog*, is a crime-supernatural yarn.

In recent years, Simon has branched out into screenwriting – collaborating with a co-writer on a script for a TV thriller under the guidance of a BAFTA-winning TV producer and co-authoring a horror movie script for Hollywood investors.

Outside writing, Simon's interests include cartooning and caricaturing (something he has enjoyed ever since he could hold a pen), playing music (having spent eight years as a drummer in various Punk bands during a somewhat mis-spent youth, Simon now plays guitar and writes songs) and playing tennis (often up to three times a week, when weather permits).

For more information about Simon and his writing, please see the following websites:

Simon's blog:

https://simoncorbin.wordpress.com/simons-blog/

Website for Simon's novel Rude Boy:

http://rudeboybook.com/

Website for Simon's novel Love, Gudrun Ensslin:

http://lovegudbook.weebly.com/

Simon's Amazon UK Author page:

http://www.amazon.co.uk/SimonCorbin/e/B0049AX2FC/ref=ntt_dp_epwbk_0

Printed in Great Britain
by Amazon.co.uk, Ltd.,
Marston Gate.